Shadow

Lands

By

Elen Sentier

A nibblebook from Rats Ink

first published in 2002 by
RATS INK
The Marshes Farmhouse
Eaton Bishop
Herefordshire HR2 9QT
Copyright ©1999 by Annie König
Illustrations copyright © 1999 by Annie König

British Library Catalogue-in-Publication Data
ISBN 1-903788-05-6

Printed in Great Britain by
Antony Rowe Limited, Eastbourne.

Contents

Coming soon by Elen Sentier

The Owl Woman

For my friends
in the Twilight Zone

Monster Mash

"The light's the thing, son" his father told him, waving the fork in his face. "All purpley and shimmering. The locals call it brillig"

They were sat in the transit café waiting for his shuttle which was late, of course. It had probably decided to be late as soon as it heard him buy his ticket. The old man swilled down his chips with a third pint and called for more while he sipped his orange juice in silence, thinking longingly of being hunched over his computer in the dusty old library where no one ever came. No point in dwelling on that, he admonished himself, that was over now. Why couldn't they have just let him be? The other sons, his elder brothers, had done all the adventuring anyone could want of their children, he was not the adventuring type. His mind rolled back to the latest web site he'd found and recalled the excitement he'd felt as he'd been about to link the site into his network. And then the summons had come.

Mum was a romantic. She loved her son, her boy, but he'd shrunk from the cloying pink atmosphere of the largest party the city had seen for a generation. Everyone had come, kissed him, shook his hand, pawed his clothing. The females fawned against him, their soft, luscious curves enfolding him until he felt buried under mountains of tit.

"Come to my arms" his mother cried over the heads of all the guests.

His mouth was covered in chocolate when they eventually dragged him out from hiding under the table with Griselda. They pushed him across the dance floor and man-handled him on to the stage. He forgot about his mouth when he saw the sword gleaming dully out of focus under the bright lights. Damn! Why had he let Griselda take his contact lenses out?

His mother towered over him, feet akimbo, wielding the yard of shining metal with a great flourish. Someone kicked him behind the knees so he grovelled before her. Grabbing her skirts to catch his balance, he grinned up weakly, confused by the flashing lights.

"I dub thee hero" she cried, whacking him on each shoulder with the monstrous blade. He had the bruises still. He tottered off with the stupid thing dangling from his belt, getting caught between his legs, Griselda smirking at his side.

The shuttle left him in a clearing and departed splattering him with mud. The pool of water at the foot ladder came over the top of his shoes. The trees stood out like dark steel against the purpley light and the mists snaking around their roots permeated his brain so he couldn't think. He trudged off through the mire.

After an hour he stopped to wipe his glasses on the end of his tie, shivering inside his Burberry and wishing Griselda had given him back his contact lenses. She said wanted to make earrings of them, as a keepsake, in case he didn't come back. He peered at the map to see but it was impossible, he had no idea where he was. The wind had dropped, the forest was eerily silent, one hand sneaked down to stroke the cloudy green jewel in the pommel of the sword.

"Jub! Jub!" the big black bird screamed from a branch right over his head. He jumped, tried to run and fell flat on his face as the sword got between his legs again and tripped him up. It came half out of its scabbard and glimmered wickedly.

"Not doing very well so far are we?" he told himself. "The trouble is, you're just not cut out for all this hero nonsense. It would be better if you just gave up and went home." He regularly gave himself good advice but rarely took it.

He tried walking in the opposite direction but the path twisted suddenly under his feet, turning him back the way he'd been going. He thought about taking the sword out to be ready and it leapt from its scabbard, gleaming malevolently at him.

"I hope you know what you're doing" he told it doubtfully. A wicked flicker of light travelled down the blade, he almost thought it was grinning at him.

He followed the path going deeper into the forest until suddenly sunlight brightened the gloom and he saw the tree standing up tall and golden in the clearing. Gratefully he stumbled towards it and sank into the soft green moss at its roots. He put the plastic water bottle to his lips and let the warm liquid ease his dry throat. Fumbling in the overcoat pockets he found the greasy packet of sandwiches and stared at them. They were very squashy and his nose twitched slightly at the ripe smell. The cheese was hot and sweaty, the cucumber had definitely faded and the lettuce hung in limp rags over the edge of the white crust. His eyes glazed over and he began to doze.

The whiffling noise penetrated his dreams as the creature made its way through the wood. It could smell the sandwiches and it was hungry. It began to burble.

He was hardly awake when the sword poked him in the ribs and leapt into his hand. One, two! One two! It went snicker-snack around his head. The creature jumped back and sat down on its haunches with its tongue hanging out like an enormous dog. They panted at each other while the sword crackled blue lightning up and down its blade. It was definitely cross.

Gingerly, never losing contact with the dark limpid pools of the creature's eyes, he reached for the scabbard. The sword guessed what he was up to and jumped out of his hand, cutting his thumb for good measure. Immediately it began the attack and the creature scuttled behind the golden tree. The sword quivered with fury.

"I say!" the creature began, hesitantly poking its snout over a branch "Does it always do that?"

"I don't know" he replied. "I only just got it."

"Isn't there anything we can do?"

Very quietly, he took off his overcoat and sneaked up behind the sword. With a yell he flung the coat, muffling the sword in the heavy cloth, and rugby tackled it to the ground. Then he sat on it, panting. The sword made a final attempt to free itself before it went quiet.

"It'll probably sulk for days" the creature remarked, sliding its head around the trunk of the tree. Its orange nostrils quivered at the smell of the sandwiches.

"If you sat on it I could try and get it back into the scabbard" he said.

The creature shot back behind the tree. After a moment its head appeared on the other side.

"D-d-d-do you think that's wise? It seems to be me it's after!"

"Oh do buck up! I don't want to be stuck here all day sitting on a sword and you don't want it chasing you through the forest."

The creature crept out and pounced on the Burberry beside him. The sword gave a terrific heave but they managed to get it back into the scabbard although it got red hot and the cloudy green jewel flashed emerald lightnings. They hung it in the golden tree where gradually it went quiet. The creature's scales were gleaming wetly and a sweet musky smell came from its armpits.

"Are you going to eat those sandwiches " it was dribbling slightly. He held out the package and it gulped them down, grease-proof paper and all.

"What do we do now?" the creature polished its turquoise fangs with a long purple tongue.

"I suppose I must go home. But I shan't have your head to show so I don't suppose they'll be very pleased with me."

"It's very dull here, in the wood" it burbled.

"What are you saying?" he asked.

"Well," it gave him a sidelong glance, "My family wanted me to be different. I've got a masters degree in computing and I'm a whiz on the internet and anyway, all the rest of my family have been killed off by heroes. I always wanted to travel ..." its voice trailed off.

Oh, lord! he thought, just my luck to get a nerd for a monster. What would his mother say if he brought it back whole, alive? He thought longingly of his computer in the library and as if it had read his mind, the creature whispered "I could help you create an inter-galactic web site ..."

Mother basked in the reflected glory of her boy. So much more interesting than ordinary heroes! Her son didn't just kill monsters, he brought his home and, between them, they transformed her City to become a knowledge base for the whole universe. He was such a clever boy!

If you want to know the whole history of monsters and their heroes, the web site is www.monsters.com . They say you can find anything there.

Big Wheel Keep on Turning

The big wheel kept on turning, the white water spread its legs wide behind, as the paddle steamer made her way luxuriously towards the pier. Jake's hands spun the roulette wheel one more time, just one more time, to get the balance right and then stopped it in its spin. He had it now. The red and black wheel would go and stop whenever he told it to.

The wooden box was rough on the silk covering her slim ass but she sat there waiting just the same. She was always waiting. The glaring yellow light from the gas lamp over her head showed lots of dark red and shadows. The old piano rumbled out the blues through the rotten wooden frames and broken windows behind her.

"Ya wanna a whisky gal?" The voice called to her over the top of the creaking pine door.

Old Tom followed up on his offer, shuffling through the swing doors whilst slopping a shot of bourbon into the greasy glass. He spilled himself onto the street night on night, but never a drop of the precious golden fluid ever hit the deck. He sat himself down on the wooden box beside her, putting the bottle on the ground. One hand proffered the whisky while the other fumbled the inside of her thigh. Small payment, she thought.

Pulling on his boots, Christian's hands caressed the soft leather.

"Like a dead woman's skin." He thought, stretching his long thin body in front of the peer glass. Tonight was his. She'd promised him that, if nothing else.

The paddle steamer came to the pier, her lights shattering the shadows and lighting Kitty into a mix of white skin and grubby scarlet silk. She took Tom's hand out of her crotch and kissed his old bald head.

"Thanks for the whisky, Tom."

"Honey, don' ya leave me now. Don't ya go!"

"Gotta work, Tom" her hand slid down his neck. "I gotta go."

He reached to catch the silk of her dress, too late as usual. He was always too late. Watching her hips slink up the gang plank he thought "Silk pussy!".

The huge saloon was in half light as Kitty came up behind Jake and slid her hand up his back.

"Hey gal!" He turned and took her waist between his hands as she slid herself up against him, licking his neck.

"Go tart up, gal" Jake reluctantly pulled away. "He'll be here soon.

Kitty's fingers lingered on his cheek, walked down to his mouth. He sucked each one in turn, then watched her shimmy away from him towards the powder room.

Christian finished his plate of catfish and opened his throat to the last of the beer in his glass. Throwing some silver on the table, he scraped the chair back and left. The innkeeper shrugged and gathered the scattered coins. He remembered Christian as a boy, tall and gangly, riding the black thoroughbred through the town or tooling his grandfather's phaeton up the main street, getting all the girls to hang out the windows. Then the old man had died and all that Christian thought was his had turned out to be mortgaged to St John. Christian's father shot himself. The first barrel missed, taking out half his neck and shoulder but stubbornly he'd managed to put the gun in his mouth and pull the trigger again. Town wits said he'd blown away the parts he never used.

The innkeeper wiped the table, piling dishes. At least the boy'd had the wit to marry St John's blind daughter. No-one else would take the girl although she carried the lure of Hartlands as dowry. To get his own back was all that Christian wanted, at least at first.

He would never leave the land, the old house with its great white Corinthian columns propping up the roof, the cotton sheds, the crumbling fields and tangled woods. He loved the place. And anyway, the innkeeper thought, he had no trade but owner and master, knew nothing of the world beyond his feudal home. The black boys he gave orders to took good care of him, although in truth they belonged to St John. For some reason they loved the gangly lad. Even Old Tom, no use now in shed or field, kept his one brown eye on the boy. One day it would all blow, the innkeeper knew it in his bones. What would Little Miss Mousy do then, sitting in the study, staring blind eyes into the sunlit garden?

The paddle steamer blew its siren. The men pushed the plank away from the side as Christian leapt for it. He landed on the deck panting. The longshoremen knew him, they smirked behind his back. Pulling his stock looser and then tighter round his neck, Christian got his breath back and strolled forward to the saloon, hands in pockets.

She wasn't there. He stood at the bar, watching in the mirror as bodies passed behind him but nowhere could he see the red silk, the cloud of black hair. He ordered more whisky. The paddle steamer heaved a little as she made her way into the great river's central channel. The boy behind the bar was new, he spilled a little of the precious fluid on the shining rosewood. Christian stood tracing patterns in the sticky liquid as the hum of gamblers and prostitutes rose around him

Suddenly her shadow crossed the mirror behind the bar, weaving through the throng of early drinkers. He pretended not to notice, keeping his eyes on the lazy

15

eight he traced back and forth in the whisky slops. But she knew.

"Waiting for me, Christian?" The small white hand covered his, his flesh tingled. "That was good of you." She piled herself gracefully onto the stool next to him.

The barman came, a bottle of Kentucky in his hand. Christian would not see, he was angry with her, with himself for wanting her. It was impossible.

"I'm thirsty, Christian" the voice was plaintive, reminding him of the blind woman at home.

"Drink water then!" he muttered churlishly, not looking at her.

She motioned the barman to pour into both glasses, nodding to his cocked eyebrow. They both knew Christian would pay in the end.

"Are you ready?" she asked him.

He knocked back the honey coloured liquid and immediately poured himself another shot.

"You can't be too drunk" she cautioned him.

He swallowed the second shot and slammed the glass down on the rosewood. Turning, he took her arm ungently, pulling her off the stool so that she stumbled and would have fallen had he not had hold of her. Her breath whistled between clenched teeth at the pain but she followed him without resistance through the crowd. They arrived at Jake's table.

St John was there, a large pile of counters already in front of him, a wry, hungry smile turning down the corners of his mouth. He didn't even look towards Christian as he said

"How much am I to vouch for you tonight, boy?"

Christian set his small rouleau down in front of him. Kitty stood by Jake, flaunting cleavage and sinuous silk. Jake spun the wheel. Black. Five. Groans ringed the table as Jake pushed more counters towards St John.

"Faites vos jeux!" Jake spun the wheel again.

Christian pushed a counter forward.

Time seemed to stop, everyone watched the wheel. Christian could hear his heartbeat below the drone of violins and the tinkling, glassy chatter. The red and the black swirled before his eyes, dragging him down into the vortex, becoming again his father's hair tangling in the blood on the wall behind the desk in the study. The blind woman sat there now every day, by the wide bay windows. That room caught the sunlight best in the old house. Christian would call to her from the doorway but never go in.

The warm, sweet smell of fresh blood rose up in his nostrils again and he gagged. A waiter was at his side with a glass and Christian came back to earth as the pungent smell of beer rose into his nostrils. He looked across the table, finding Kitty's eyes veiled but watching him. The little finger of her left hand flicked outwards. He pushed a large counter onto the black seven. Jake spun the wheel, smiling faintly into his moustache.

"Even the feeble idiot is favoured by fortune's wheel on occasion" St John drawled as the wheel stopped. "Don't lose it all 'til I come by again boy!" and he pushed a handful of counters onto the eleven.

The wheel kept on turning. Drinks flowed around the table, passing Christian by. Brittle laughter and sparkling conversation danced but there was a circle of darkness around him which his neighbours dared not enter. St John's wit lacerated it on occasion but could not break the spell. Christian found himself suspended in time. His glassy eyes alternated between watching the flick of Kitty's fingers and the maelstrom of red and black within the wheel. The pile of counters sank and rose and sank again in front of him. The hands of the clock crawled towards dawn. He pushed forward a counter in obedience to Kitty's signal.

Why did he trust her? She was Jake's. She would never be his however much he wanted, however much money he had. It was Jake she wanted, Jake she held in her heart while she held his cock between her legs. He knew it as surely as all the other men. The wheel turned.

St John's pile had risen high. It flowed out to encroach his neighbours' space. They carefully drew in their own small winnings. No-one would dispute with St John. Each carefully guarded his own meagre stock from falling by accident into that gross pile. Once there, they knew too well, the money would never return home. Oh, sometimes it seemed that counters would escape to, holiday awhile in another man's pile but sooner or later they would hear the call and return to their master. St John never allowed straying and punishment was dire.

A waiter appeared with a tall, foaming glass on his tray. Christian sniffed at it, looking up at the boy with a puzzled stare.

"The lady said she felt you needed refreshing sir."

The waiter smirked at Christian, nodding backwards towards a thin, elderly woman in black lace. Bemused, Christian caught the old woman's eye as she smiled faintly. He let his own glance fall. He sipped the chilled liquid, allowing the champagne bubbles to float through his system somehow enlivening him. The flicker of Kitty's fingers brought him back to earth. He set down the glass and pushed the whole of his pile onto the red thirteen.

"Don't let it go to your head, boy!" St John barked "the old dame's drunk again. She always was your father's whore!"

Christian's hand was steady as he laid the counters down. The baiting was hardly more than usual. He must not be angry now. He looked up, staring defiantly at the older man like a child awaiting a whipping.

Satisfied his son-in-law was cowed, St John glared around the table. There was little left now before each of the players, many were already beggared at his hand. The pink skirts of dawn brushed the cabin windows. St John took a deep breath and pushed all his pile onto the black then let his eyes rest on the large pile in front of his son in law. It would be pleasant to take the last shreds of hope from the boy, yet again.

Jake spun the wheel. He could feel it move under his hands. This was his moment, whatever the morrow should bring.

The strain of the evening was telling on Christian. He could feel himself falling again into the vortex. What did it matter anyway? Everything was lost. The dreams of the boy riding the black stallion his father had said no-one would ever tame were long gone. Even the horse had been in his grave a good few years.

The red leaves of fall slapped his cheeks, the black branches of wintering trees snagged his coat but none could stop them. The horse flew through the forest, needing no more than a touch on the side of the neck from the reins. Together they drove through the tunnel of autumn towards the bright darkness. At the end of the ride, he knew, would be his father's bloody head splattered over the study wall.

The wheel slowed. The silver ball rattled up and down, up and down, across the numbers. Gradually Christian rose out of the vortex. The wheel stopped.

" Red thirteen!" cried Jake. "Unlucky for some!" he sneered at St John.

Cries of delight rose from the table. People crowded up to see, other players broke through the dark circle into Christian's space, slapping his shoulder and taking his hand. Drink flowed around him again. Even the old woman hobbled over and took his hand, her twisted limbs belying the beauty of her ancient face.

Jake pushed the pile of counters across the table to Christian. Many hands helped the tumbled coins find their new home with the young man. Someone opened windows and the smell of warm, wet river rose around them. Sunlight sparked on the bright metal in his hand.

"Don't let me find you here again, boy!" The harsh crow's voice broke through the joyous carolling of the other gamblers. St John lurched out.

The paddle steamer tied up again beside the rotting pier. The gamblers left, the prostitutes counted their cash before the pimps arrived to strip it from them. Christian stood bemusedly in the centre of the saloon.

"Now!" said Kitty. "Go on. You know what you have to do."

His head jerked as he drew himself up. to his full height Looking down he swallowed her with his eyes as though it was the last time.

Outside he could hear the footsteps ahead of him in the morning quiet. He walked between tar barrels, ropes and tumbling sheds, following the dark figure through the edge of the town, into the woods. His soft leather boots made no sound. He walked in another world.

At the crossing it was easy. He came up silently behind the St John, the rushing river sounds concealed his stealthy boots. The stones were slippery. He was not even sure he actually touched the older man's shoulder but he heard the cry as St John slipped and fell. His head hit the stepping stone, breaking open, leaking the pretty scarlet fluid into the water. It swirled, reminding him of her dress. He walked quickly back into town.

The innkeeper had his breakfast ready for him. "Heard about your winning, sir."

The beer and eggs arrived although he didn't want them. He stirred the mess of yolk and white around the plate awhile, unable to get any into his mouth.

He wandered back out into the street, forgetting to pay for the food. Nobody seemed to mind.

Kitty was leaning against the railings of the observation car, watching the silver tracks sliding back away from the train wheels when she heard Jake come out of the door behind her.

"What will he do?" She said, not looking at him. "He hates her you know."

"Do?" Jake put his hands around her waist and leaned into the cloud of black hair. "He'll take back his lands. It's not our business any more, honey. We got our own future ahead of us. Come on back inside now" and he drew her into the drawing room car.

"Who's there? Who is that? Christian! Tell me it's you!" her voice shrilled as she heard him enter the study but he didn't answer. "The doctor called last night, while you were out. He says it's true." Her voice caught, her hands fluttered like pale moths in the sun.

The morning sun peered through the windows of the New York apartment lighting the paper Jake had thrown down on the sofa when he went out. The page was torn and in straightening it she saw the name.

"Second Tragedy Hits Dunbar." Kitty read the headline of the small paragraph.

"Not a year after the terrible death of his father-in-law Christian Dunbar today mourns the loss of his young wife." Kitty laid the paper down on her lap, looking across the room into another space.

"The body of Davinia Dunbar, daughter of wealthy merchant Wilbur St John, was found by her maid yesterday at the bottom of the stairs. Dunbar, who was away buying horses at the Kentucky fair, was told by wire later that same morning. He is beside himself. Not only has he lost his dear wife but she was carrying their first child. The accident happened …."

Kitty stopped reading. She went into the bedroom and began to pack.

The big wheel kept on turning. Kitty shaded her eyes to watch the white water spread its legs wide behind until its toes touched the shores on either side. The linen covered cushions on the steamer chair were easy on the black silk covering her slim ass. The yellow sun shone through the whiskey in her glass making long evening shadows of her fingers across the deck. Behind her the piano sang the blues through the rosewood windows.

In the distance she saw his shadow move across the pier. It wouldn't be long now.

Spirit Cat

The sun shining down on her bare neck was hot, really hot. Turning her head upwards the sky was dark, deep, burning blue light, over head the brazen sun was impossible to look at except when mirrored in the deep pool at her knees. The grass was slippery dry and sharp, silvery, even the young May-green leaves on the trees had a silvery tinge. It was as though the colour was leached out of everything in the fierce sunlight, without a breeze to move the air. There was no sound or ripple to disturb her thoughts but she didn't want to think. There was a tiny splash and the water in front of her rippled, she was crying again.

The pool was deep. Some said it reached down to the roots of the world-tree, bringing its water up from Segais, the well-spring of the world. It was feared now in the village since the woman had come, telling of the fearsome dark and the wild things that lived there with no love for men. But to her it was a hidden sanctuary where she could come when she was afraid, alone. She held herself tightly in her own arms, rocking, moaning quietly although she could not hear herself. Things had been so different whilst her mother lived.

Lost in her thoughts, she jumped. The cat was there again, black and sleek. He was busy today, pushing against her hand, chirruping softly in his throat as though calling to her. She watched him, excited, fearful. It was rare to see a cat these days, none came to the village any more. He walked away a few paces then turned, looking back at her over his shoulder, chirruping again.

"What is it? Do you want me to come with you?"

Again the chirrup, watching, waiting for her, until she is ready. Rising she followed his path to where he disappeared in among the trees, and there she stopped.

Catching her breath in a ripple of fear, she started as the low ferns moved and there he was again. The path wound out in front of them, a velvet of short rabbit-bitten grass, showing no footprints.

"I can't go in there" she told him, her mind torn between her stepmother's injunction and the memory of her real mother carrying her amongst the gentle light filtering through the trees. He twined himself about her legs again, walking round behind, butting her so hard she stumbled forward and her feet were on the forest path. The turf was springy, pleasant underfoot.

He continued to butt, gently pushing her forward step by step, until they were some way into the forest, then he passed continuing up the track, turning to see if she would follow. She turned her head to see the way they had come and ... nothing, no path at all, nothing but bracken, high and stiff, tall as her waist.

She turned back to him feeling a cold hand gripping her heart, as her stepmother had said she would. Turning she could see ahead, the path winding gently in and out amongst the trees, ferns and soft grasses parting here and there to show the summer flowers. She turned again. Behind stood the wall of bracken, last years dried fronds untouched by any living thing, dry and sharp and stiff, high and impenetrable, barring her way. The cat wound himself widdershins about her legs again. He caught her eyes and the cold receded, she found she could feel her blood pulsing in time with his purring. The breath she had been holding now for seeming hours, years, sighed out of her and she drew in a lung-full of clean, damp forest smell and the faint odour of wood-smoke. He stepped out ahead and now she followed unresisting, she was helpless in the journey, she had been taken, had surrendered herself to that taking, not knowing what would come of it.

The path wove in amongst the trunks, narrow, confined by ancient trees. She would slip between the silver birch, duck under the twisted boughs of oak until they reached the stream. He waited, sitting on the centre of the log. She laughed, picked up her skirts and danced across into the dappled glade full of the scent of May. Peaceful, it was difficult to be afraid hearing the birds at their lazy chirping, watching a hare quietly nibbling grass in the shade of a tree. They had no concern for her presence. She followed, trusting in his path.

The wood-smoke smell was stronger now, she could see the outlines of a cottage through the leaves and suddenly the trees opened up. She came up all standing, watching the sun sparkle off the white cob walls, the spiral of smoke rising out the centre of the roof. The cat disappeared into the inviting darkness of the doorway. A moment later the man came out and crossed the clearing towards her.

"Thirsty?" he smiled down at her. She nodded, he took her hand.

Inside was dark and cool, out of sight of the burning sun. An earthenware pot on the table sweated drops of moisture cooling the liquid within. He dipped a ladle into water and filled a cup. He held it to her. She put her hands behind her back and stepped away from him.

"See" he said as he put the cup to his lips, swallowed, then held it out to her again. Water dripped from his lips. Watching him, she knew the sinking feeling as something ended and began within her, but her thirst drew her and she took the cup, drank, swallowing the knowledge that there was no going back. Going outside, she sat with him in the shade, knowing him a little. The hare came to nuzzle her hand, look up into her eyes.

She told him how her mother died, her father married again, this time a woman from the east who brought new customs. She told of the sacrifices, the cats burning in baskets each May-tide to ensure a good harvest. And the woman would also burn them alone in secret to get her auguries, waiting until the creature's screaming pain drew down the spirit-cat who would give her answers to spare his creature's pain. There were no cats now around the village, the rats and mice eating the grain from what little harvest the village could muster since the woman had come. He heard her.

"She hates me too" she told him "she would kill me if she could." He held her. The hare watched them, still and quiet in the grass.

"I must go." She said, leaving him. But she came again next day, and the next, following the black cat along the forest path. He would wait for her at the hidden pool, and walk with her, always entering the cottage before her,, announcing her arrival. She never saw them together.

In the long afternoons, while the hay was ripening, they would roll together on the grass in front of the cottage like lions at play. After a month she could feel the life quicken inside her.

Hay harvest came. The men took out their scythes cleaning, sharpening, singing the old songs over them. Still she walked the fields each day, unknowing she had a watcher. Kai, her step-brother, followed when his mother told him, but only so far. It was easy across the fields, watching from the hedgerow but he would not enter the forest, never found the path. But he would watch her go in, her tread heavy and fearful. And he would see her return, light of step.

He was there the day the men took their scythes to cut the hay. He watched them build the stooks, creeping between and hiding in the one nearest the forest. He knew what his mother had told them. The men must be on guard, cut down anything that came from the forest whatever it's shape, for the fay ones would send the White Mare to destroy the harvest and bring bad luck. The men believed, since she had shown them the Mari Llwyd at the festival of sun-return, the skeleton horse who danced and bit to find the one who could not get out of the way, the one who would bear the beating for the village. Last year it had been him.

Kai watched the men through the day, cutting and binding. He saw her cross the fields, enter the forest, whilst the men were at their mid-day meal, unheeding. He waited fasting, licking his cracked lips for thirst, tasting the salt of his sweat, knowing he could not move until she should return.

As the sun climbed down the sky the light altered, heavy black clouds rolled up out of the west, darkening the sky and casting purple shadows among the hay cocks. Nothing seemed clear or real in the strange shifting light. The men hastened wanting to finish their work, fearing a storm. They came to the last stook and, standing in a circle, began to toss their scythes for who should make the last cut, the unlucky cut, the mare's neck. The lot fell on the youngest man, a boy of Kai's age. Fearful, he began his work and she walked out of the wood. In the fading light of the coming storm she seemed as dainty as a young filly, walking across the stubble, her head held high. Kai leapt up with a cry, calling the men,

"The Mare! The White Mare! The White Mare comes" and he rushed towards her.

The men followed, scythes raised, crying out in fear and anger at sight of the White Mare. They were on her in the instant, blades flashing down silver, rising up red. She was cut and cut and cut again.

And then the men began to see again, one wiped his face with a bloody hand, licked his now red lips, tasted her. And then they saw what they had done, the limbs twisted and broken, the fair skin ravaged and bloody. And another madness took them. They dropped the bloody scythes and fell on Kai, rending, tearing him with the strength of their hands until there was nothing recognisably human left.

Breathless, panting out their fear and horror, they stopped, listening. Claws of lightning ripped through the purple clouds, the low yowling roar of the thunder grew, striding across the sky closer and closer.

They fled the horror behind them, running for their lives towards the terror in the village ahead.

She heard the thunder where she worked within the hut, saw the pots and kettles silvered in the lightning flash but the sound of running feet never reached her. They dragged her out by the hair. Screaming curses, she clawed at them but they held her down.

"This for Tanith" each one said as he began his ride of the white mare.

Then they gathered torches, fired the walls and threw her back into the blazing pyre and sat down, waiting. Would the spirit cat answer her howling?

He heard the cries as he padded across the field to where she lay. Sitting beside the bloody remains he listened again for the mewling. Reaching inside, he lifted out the tiny kitten, placed her on a patch of dry earth and licked away the blood from the soft white fur. She hung purring peacefully from his powerful jaws as he carried her home into the forest.

At sun-return the villagers took the white bones, the horse skull, and burned them to ashes. They watched as the white cat came heavy and slow to the fire, warming herself at the blaze. The old man made a nest for her to birth in and later, at Brighid's fire, he gave each harvester a kitten.

Sitting vigil at the fire, the men knew they were not alone, a deep throbbing sound came from hearth, they sensed warm fur brushing their skin as they dozed, and one man saw two pairs of glowing golden eyes watching from the other side of the fire. But when he got up to look there was nothing there.

The Pig-Sty Prince and the Giant's Daughter

I tell'ee! Have nothin' to do wi'it!

Culhwch could hear the voice still, echoing down the long tree-bound ride but he would not listen to it. The old one stood in the doorway shaking his staff, willing his young charge to stop but knowing, all the while, it was to no avail.

Culhwch ducked the low branches which threatened to sweep him off the horse as his horse's hooves thudded into the green turf, his mind still on the dream. Every night now, since the feast of his return, the same dream. The same gold-bronze hair tied back with a velvet band which matched the blue of her eyes. Now everywhere he looked he saw her.

His mind went back to the night of the feast. His father's wife had leaned towards him so that the dark crystal swung lose from between the white mounds of her breasts. It swung to and fro, to and fro, mesmerising.

"Will ye not marry my daughter, Culhwch?" she said.

"No!" his voice was thick with disgust as he answered her. "No, I will not."

After the third asking she had sat back in the high chair. Her fingers danced softly over the mellow wood, along the edge of the pewter plate. His eyes followed. She sang softly in her throat but the words made no sense to him.

He felt lost here in the wide hall. The soft light shone through the windows, the smell of food was sweetly overpowering and the people, he had never been among so many people in his life. His heart turned longingly back to the old white sow with her brood of piglings snuffling amongst the beechmast in the clearing. Sometimes she would turn up truffles for him, at others lead him to a hazel grove where the forest floor was carpeted with nuts. He would collect them and bring them home to the Old One of an evening. They would sit together beside the fire while the great pig suckled her little ones in the sty next door. Quiet it had been, not like this great hall.

The man he now called father he could hardly remember. There was an image there, a sense of the movement of a horse beneath him, a strong brown arm about him and a voice.

"Take care of him!" the voice had said. And he was alone with the bent old man and his pig, the sound of thudding hooves receding into the distance.

"Your mother ran mad, boy, had you heard tell?"

The honey-voice had called him back into the great hall. His father's wife was leaning towards him again, the heavy scent of apricots cloyed his mind. Her teeth were very white.

"She ran mad, boy, just as her time came on her. Ran into a pig-sty and birthed you out into the mire. Did you know that boy?"

"Culhwch! The pig-sty prince!" His father's wife's daughter laughed, a tinkling sound, like icicles cracking in the morning sun. Her cold white hand touched his.

"Never worry it, mother dear. I find I do not like the smell of pigs in my bed!"

That night the dream had come the first time. A slender woman, red-gold hair falling like a sheet of water down her back, tied back from her brow with a sapphire coloured band. Her coral lips smiled to him and she held out her hand. Then something caught her eye and she looked back over her shoulder in fear. Something huge and dark approached them out of the cold night and he awoke. On the third night he heard her name called on the wind, "Olwen! Olwen!".

He woke with the word on his own lips.

"There's none hereabouts knows aught of her," his father told him as they walked together through the dim mews. "Go to the great court, my son. Arthur and his men will know if any do. And they will help you."

It wasn't really on his way but he had gone back again to his foster-home, the pig-sty and to his foster-father, the old one, to tell his tale again.

"Don't go! Have nothing to do with it!" the old one insisted but Culhwch didn't listen.

The trees thinned. The country all about became more open and gradually, like a cloud resting upon the hilltop, he began to make it out. The towers and spires grew out of the very rock like the ridges on a dragon's back, seeming to float and change their shape like clouds in a gentle wind. He watched the light move round and down until it lit the towers from below so they loomed blue-black against the rose coloured sky. The last red flash of sun lit his horse's silver coat as he walked wearily up to the gate.

"What want ye here?!"

He didn't see the gnarled shape of the door-keeper at first. A twisted hand took the bridle rein and stopped the horse in his tracks.

"What want ye here?!" came the challenge again. "Say out your business for I like not the look of ye. What want ye here?"

"I seek the maiden, Olwen". Culhwch squinted down through the last rays of sun into the dark face.

"Faugh! Get ye gone, stupid boy! We want none of ye here!"

Culhwch got a grip on himself and gentling back the reins he made the horse stand up and paw the air with sharp hooves. The door-keeper dropped back a pace.

"I have the silver tongue!" Culhwch sang. "I will cry satire on the king else you stand back and let me in."

The door-keeper stood aside. As he passed, Culhwch thought he saw a smile creasing the leathery skin but it might have been a trick of the light.

In the hall of the great king Culhwch went straight to Arthur's feet.

"Sire, trim my hair for me, for I am of thy kin."

Arthur looked and saw that Culhwch was indeed of the kindred and he said to him

"Anything canst though have save only my horse, my hound, my fighting gear and my wife. What will'st thou of me, kindred son?"

"Grant me the boon to find the lady Olwen for my bride I ask it in the names of all the knights and all the ladies at this court."

And Arthur granted it. He sent out all the knights to search valiantly for a year and a day but nothing could they find and Culhwch was angry. He came to Arthur saying

"Th'art a promise breaker, King of kings. I am a bard and I will rhyme thee and cry satire on thy house and all within it."

"Nay, lad, go out now with my men, I give thee Cynddilyd for thy guide to who all lands are known, and Gwrthyr for interpreter to whom all tongues are as his own, and Gwalchmai who accomplishes every quest he undertakes, and Menw who is master of every kind of magic, and Bedwyr who never shies from any exploit. And I give you Cei, for the powers of Cei are such that he can hold one breath within his lungs for nine days and nights, any wound he gives is beyond all healers' arts and herbs, he can be shadow or light or seem as tall as a tree an' so he wills."

So Culhwch travelled with this company until one day they came upon a great mound where sat a giant herdsman. He was taller than the hills and broader than the rivers and deeper than the crystal caves. And beside him sat his dog who was himself greater than an elephant, while down below then were a great herd of sheep more numerous than the white hawthorn blossom in May.

"Go speak to him," said Culhwch to Gwrthyr.

"Nay! Not I! He is too large for me and what about the dog?!"

"I've a magic greater than a leash for Arawn's hounds, I'll spell him w'it," said Menw.

"And I stand in the shadow behind thee." said Cei.

And so, cautiously, Gwrthyr, approached the hill.

"Greetings herdsman! Who art thou and whose sheep are these that you guard so vigilantly?" Cried Gwrthyr of the many tongues.

The giant herdsman leaned way down from the top of his hill and sent forth a breath of flame which singed Gwrthyr's beard and set his horse to running. The others backed off a bit but didn't leave the field.

"Why these are the sheep of my brother Yspaddaden and I am Custennin who guards these sheep and these lands from all comers. And whose sheep are ye?" called down the herdsman from the top of his hill eyeing them closely, for he was used to people leaving him alone once he had breathed fire upon them.

"We come from Arthur's court upon great quest" said Gwrthyr. "Know'st aught of the maiden Olwen?" they cried.

"Aye!" the giant herdsman leaned down towards them. All seven knights backed up their horses quickly. "Aye, I knows of Olwen. And where she steps the white clovers spring up in her path for she is called, the Maiden of the White Track. What want'st thee with her?"

"She is my promised bride." Culhwch shouted back, pushing his way through the others. And the giant laughed and laughed and laughed.

"Aye! Happen so? Then 'tis Yspaddaden ye'll be dealin' with." said the herdsman when he could catch his breath. "Yspaddaden! Aye, I know him all too well, my brother. It is because of my wife that he has taken my lands and eaten all my children save for Goreu who we hide in a chest. It is because of my lovely wife he forces me to serve him in this place!" The herdsman's brow beetled.

"Why how is this?" Gwrthyr asked.

"A long story," he replied. "Enough that he has taken my place and my lands and my children. What pledge have ye to give me that I may know thee?"

And Culhwch handed him an arm ring and straight way the herdsman came down from his mound and scooped Culhwch off his horse and into his beard, saying "Th'art my nephew boy, my wife's sister's son. Come I will help thee." And they went back with him to his house and were feasted there.

"Tomorrow night" the herdsman's wife said. "For tomorrow is Saturday and every Saturday Olwen comes to me to wash her hair and so you shall see her." And so it came about that he stood at last before the golden-bronze haired maiden, looking into her deep blue eyes.

"I cannot marry you," she said, "For I have promised my father. And if I marry then he will die."

"But what am I to do?" cried Culhwch. "For now I have found you I will never part from you again."

"You must come with me and ask him for my hand." She replied. "He cannot refuse you but he will set you tasks. Whatever tasks he sets you, you must agree to accomplish, no matter how impossible they seem."

So they came with Olwen into her father's hall, where they found the nine gates guarded by the nine porters and the nine great hounds. Culhwch and his friends called the potters and then killed them as they stood at their gates and the hounds along with them. And so they entered into the giant's castle. Yspaddaden was a giant even larger than Custennin the herdsman and he sat at his table half asleep.

"I come to ask for the hand of Olwen, your daughter, in marriage," cried Culhwch as bravely as he could.

Lifting himself from the board Yspaddaden called his servant. "Ho there! Come to me you whining snivelling wretch! Bring a pitchfork and lift my eyelid so that I may see these invaders of my hall."

And so it was done.

And when he saw Culhwch he thought to himself what a pesky little man he was. So, reaching out one hand, he took a poisoned spear and flung it at his guests. But Bedwyr caught it and flung it back at the giant, wounding him in the knee.

"I will have your daughter's hand!" cried Culhwch was angry now.

"By damn!" said Yspaddaden, "that smarts! I'll not walk easy now for the rest of my life. I'll teach the uncivil boy-child a lesson!" And he cast a second spear. But this time Menw caught it and cast it back again, catching the giant in the hollow under his ribs.

"Give me Olwen for my bride!" shouted Culhwch.

"Ouch!" cried Yspaddaden. "The wretched man has knocked me sideways! Now I'll be short of breath every day for the rest of my life!" And he caught a third poisoned spear and cast it straight at Culhwch.

But this time Culhwch caught the spear and threw it back, piercing the giant's eyeball.

Yspaddaden blinked and blinked and blinked and then the spear fell out his eye. The giant wiped his eye again and again with a rag the size of one of Prydwen's sails but he could not stop it watering.

"A cur to have as a son-in-law!" he spluttered. "I'll not see the sun rise easy of a morning again for the rest of my life and the wind will always be having my eye to watering. What a curse to live with to the end of my days!" But then he turned to Culhwch and said

"Aye! Aye! Aye! Olwen shall indeed be thy bride. But first thou must perform the anoethu, the impossible tasks." And his yellow teeth peered out from round the blackened gums as he smiled to himself, for he knew no man could do the things that he would ask and so he would have Culhwch for his breakfast.

"The stake of my play is this, and I lay it as crosses and spells that thy head and thy neck are forfeit an thou does't not fulfil these tasks. And only when you have accomplished them will you marry my daughter. And I tell you now that you will not accomplish them, for they are tasks that no man may accomplish!" And Yspaddaden chuckled long and hard for he knew that there was no way that Culhwch would be able to do these things.

"Tell on, then, father-in-law," said Culhwch. "Tell me the tale of these anoethu."

So Yspaddaden began to sing.

"Thou must root up all the hill yonder and plough it and sow it all in one day. And in one day the wheat must ripen for only from that wheat will the bread for my daughter's wedding be baked."

"Not hard, not hard to do, at all!" cried Culhwch, remembering what Olwen had said to him.

"So it may be!" sang Yspaddaden, "But there are only two men in the whole world who can till the land and rid it of its stones and they will not work for you! And the man who has the only oxen who can draw the plough to till will not give these oxen to you and you will not be able to get them. And when I did marry Olwen's mother nine bushels of flax were sown yet not a blade came up. You must recover that flax and sow it again in the wild land tilled by the men who will not work for you, ploughed by the oxen you cannot get. For it is only from this flax that the linen for my daughter's head-dress can be made."

"Not hard, not hard to do at all," said Culhwch far more bravely than he felt.

"So you may say!" sang Yspaddaden. "But there are other things that must be done as part of the anoethu and you cannot do them. I must have the honey that is nine times sweeter than ordinary honey to make the marriage drink. And I must have the Grail cup of which all the stories are told to hold this sweet wedding draught. And I must have the Cauldron of Plenty into which any man may dip his hand and draw out what he loves best of all. And you must bring me the fairy horn to pour the wine for the guests, and the fairy harp which plays without a bard to strum it to make music for the feast. And the fairy pot which boils meat without a fire to make the food for the guests."

"These things are not hard for me at all" said Culhwch in a strong voice but his heart was in his boots.

"Aye! I've heard you say so before!" The giant almost spat at Culhwch in his rage. "But I must wash my head and shave my beard and these things I cannot do without I have the blood of the jet black witch and the razor which hangs between the tusks of the great boar, Twrch Trwyth. and him you will never capture."

"Not hard, not hard at all," shouted Culhwch, angry at last with the rigmarole the giant was giving him.

"And then," Yspaddaden shouted back at him, " and then I will need the fairy comb and the fairy scissors which hang between the ears of Twrch Trwyth. and these you will never get!"

"It will be perfectly easy for me to do all of these things!" cried Culhwch in a towering rage.

"To do them," sang Yspaddaden, "you will need the fairy hounds and the fairy leash and the greatest huntsman in the world. And that is Mabon, son of Modron, who was stolen from his mother when he was only three days old and has never been seen since! And him you cannot find!" Yspaddaden sat back in his chair and waited, having come to the end of the anoethu.

"Not hard at all! Not hard at all! It will be very easy for me to find Mabon and do all of these things!" Culhwch said to him.

"Then you must get me the Glaive of Light, the sword which belongs to the King of the Oak Windows and this can only be done by killing the King with the Glaive. No other way will you get the sword from him. And this I know you cannot do."

"I will get the Glaive of Light and I will kill the King of the Oak Windows and when I have done this, then I will then take your life with the Glaive itself." Now Culhwch was cold in his anger and his eyes burned like blue ice-fire in under his dark brow.

That evening Culhwch came to Olwen with his head and his heart hanging low, for he knew not how he was to get the Glaive of Light away from the King of the Oak Windows, let alone any of the other deeds he had promised himself to do.

"You have no cause to mind that," she told him. "You have the best wife who has the best horse in the whole wide world and if you will heed me you will come well out of this." And next morning she saddled up her own dun filly for him and kissed him saying "I need tell thee nothing for the horse knows all and she will help thee."

And Culhwch kissed Olwen and rode off leaving the rest of the tasks to his companions. The filly ran so fast that she left the March wind behind her and outstripped the winds in front of her. It seemed no time at all before they got to the Castle of the King of the Oak Windows.

The dun filly slid to a halt.

"Now then," she said, "we are here. And if you listen to my words you will carry away the Sword of Light. Come now to yon window and there you'll see the Sword with a knob at its end. Lean in now and draw it gently through the window."

And Culhwch did as he was bid and the sword came to him in his hand but as its point passed the window frame so it whispered out.

"'Tis no stoppin' here for us now," said the dun filly. "For I know the King of the Oak Windows has felt the sword a-leaving of him." And she turned about as fast as fast and sped off for home.

After a little while the filly paused and said,

"Look behind us and tell me what you do see."

"I see a great host of brown horses coming madly," he answered.

"No worry then, we're faster than they," and she sped on for home.

After a little while more the filly paused again.

"What see ye now?" she asked.

And Culhwch turned and looked again. "It is a crowd of black horses coming madly," he said. And the filly turned about saying again

"Not time to worry yet for we are faster than they," and she flew on for home.

A little while again and the filly paused. "Look again, Culhwch, and what d'ye see?"

Culhwch screwed up his eyes "I see a black horse with a white face," he said "he comes on madly and madly."

"'Tis my brother," said the dun filly. "And he is the fastest horse in all the land. He will come past us like a flash of light. As they pass, try if you can cut off the head of the rider for it is the King of the Oak Windows and only the sword in your hand can cut off his head."

And Culhwch did as the dun filly told him, leaning out to full stretch, and so he sliced off the head of the King of the Oak Windows.

At last they reached the giant herdsman's home and set aside carefully the Glaive of Light where none could reach it. And Culhwch found that the men had come and the oxen been loaned and the fields had been tilled, the wheat and flax grown, the bread baked and the headdress woven all with the aid of his friends.

Next morning early the band of seven set out to find Mabon. They went first to the Blackbird of Cilgwri, Gwri's Retreat, who told them that he knew nothing of their quest but directed them to the Stag who was far older than him. The Stag of the Redynfr, Fernbrake Hill, said he too knew nothing of Mabon but told them to visit the Owl of Cawlwyd the Wood of Caw the Grey, who was older still than he and might be able to help them. The Owl again knew not of their quest but directed them to the Eagle Gwern Abwy: the Alder swamp, who was older far than he. the Eagle had heard of Mabon and he at last directed them on to find the Salmon of Llyn Llyw, the Lake of the Leader, where they would find good help. The Salmon knew Mabon and he took Cei and Gwrthyr on his shoulders to the castle where Mabon lamented in his prison. Cei fought the guards and freed Mabon and brought him back with them.

Mabon led them on the Faerie hunt with the faerie hound after the great boar. And Twrch Trwyth led them a long chase across Ireland and Cornwall until eventually they overcame him. They took the razor and the comb and the scissors from Twrch Trwyth and drove him into the sea, since when none has heard of him again, or anyroad not for certain.

The band of friends returned at last to Yspaddaden's castle, bearing the Hallows. The giant watched as they brought up each one to show him and finally he smiled the smile of satisfaction and said

"Now then, my heroes bold. Bring forth the blood of the jet black witch and wash my hair. Comb me with the fairy comb and trim my hair for me, son-in-law. Then I will be shaved as I commanded with the razor from between the tusks of Twrch Trwyth."

And so it was done. Yspaddaden was bathed and combed, trimmed and shaved according to his wishes, ready for the wedding. Then out from the chest where he had hidden away came Goreu, Yspaddaden's nephew and the son of the giant herdsman Custennin. And Culhwch gave into his hand the Glaive of Light whereupon Yspaddaden bowed down his head and Goreu cut it off.

They feasted then, long after Culhwch bedded Olwen. And Summer followed Spring, as it has done since the sun first rose into the sky

Fuji en Provençe!

Maurice sucked his brush again, by now his mouth was wholly black with ink.

Alex had given up holding the pose some while back, she lay in a damp heap on the cool floor, hardly breathing. With her back to him the rise of her hip shadowed the shape of the mountain outside the window.

Maurice looked out the window. Ventoux was wreathed in cloud, a thunderhead, crackling, waiting to happen. August in Provençe, hot. Hot skin, hot air, hot loins - but not when he looked at Alex. He got up, went over to the sink, sloshed warm white wine in a couple of tooth mugs, took one to the girl. She lifted off the red tiles, heavy thighs leaving a damp imprint.

He walked over to the window, breathing in the hot, damp air. A gasp of wind rustled the paper beside his chair, turning over the first of the drawings. He picked it up, regarding the sparse, spare, empty white space enclosed in a few black lines which went to make up the naked figure. A whole life, bounded in trailing ink. The first was always the best, every day. A heap of paper, a heap of lives, yet every one the same. Three years in a Zen monastery under Mount Fuji and what had he come to? Nudes. Nudes in Provençe forsooth!

There was still a mountain. Ventoux was very beautiful, but it was not Fuji. Add the cottage, and the wine, a far cry from the clean lines, the patient, perfect garden, the still hours of Za-Zen.

How far away that seemed now. And why had he come here, come home? If you could call it home. The parents were dead, none of the villagers remembered in him the scruffy boy who had fought and played with their sons. Attempts at friendship in the local cafes had brought only the misery of buying drinks. He was

43

suffered because he bought drinks. He'd given it up. Now he lived on bread and cheese and olives. And wine, of course, always the wine.

Alex had been passing through, was that two years ago now? They didn't speak much any more. They didn't screw much either come to that. But every day, religiously, like the Za-Zen meditations, he chewed the ends of his bamboo stick brushes, ground and mixed the ink. And he drew her. Any which way. Lying, standing, sitting, squatting, he didn't care. A few lines that's all it took and there she was on paper. Or was she? Was it monsters he was drawing, or mountains. Maurice swallowed the warm wine.

Sitting under the fig tree, after supper, he thought of her. He could hear her swilling dishes in the sink, singing to the tinny radio, some sugary song about l'amour. She always sang just too loud and off key, he hadn't noticed it at first.

He'd been sat at the end of the lane, two summers back when the Morgan pulled up. The man was angry. He, leaned over the back of the seat, pulled out the rainbow coloured bag and slung it into the dust at Maurice's feet. He had taken the girl by the arm, pushed her over the low side door of the open car. Once sure she was clear, he had driven off, leaving her sitting in the road, her short skirt hitched round her backside, blood mixing with the dust as it flowed down her leg. Maurice was surprised she wasn't crying.

He had patched her up, fed her, offered her the couch. Later, he had still been awake to hear her creep up the stairs, feel her hand stroking what was left of his grizzled pate. She had led in those days. He was surprised he still had it in him.

His drawing had changed from then on. No more of the landscapes, the hot blue trees swirling into a blue sky, attempting Van Gogh. He had returned to the black ink of Fuji, chewing his own brushes from the bamboo that grew down by the river. At first she had even found him cross legged on the veranda attempting meditation, stiff and cold, unable to move in the wet chill of an October dawn. She had laughed, kindly, rubbed his legs with Rosemary oil, brought a blanket and hot coffee. Of course it hadn't lasted.

She had been warm for him that winter, laughing into spring and lazing in the shallows of the river through the summer. With the autumn, the old disease had come back, chills and shivering, the ague. But she stayed. Now it was crawling towards autumn again. He felt she would leave before Christmas and better too for her than staying to nurse a crippled artist who couldn't even get it up.

The sun woke him eventually, shining in his face. He knew it must be late because his window faced south never catching the sun until mid morning. She was gone from his side although he remembered her tenderness last night, a rare and treasured gift. He creaked down the stairs into the kitchen, finding the coffee she had left him. There were voices out on the veranda, carefully he peered down the passage, across the living room. He could see her back, sitting at the table a heap of paper in front of her and at her side. A male voice asked a question. He padded quietly towards them on bare feet.

He could see the man now, dark, Latin features, he had seen him somewhere, the gallery in Aix which imported the modern Japanese paintings. What was the girl up to? She had heard him now, turning she smiled and called him to join them.

"André came while you were meditating still, I didn't disturb you."

Maurice wiped the back of his hand across his mouth, feeling the coagulated sleep still clinging to his eyelashes, could he look the part? He sat with his back to the sun, his grey locks to hanging forward across his face. The fig tree cast grateful shadows.

André was carefully sorting through his drawings of the past years. There was a pile of the Van Gogh clones on the floor by his feet but the drawings of Alex were on the table. He too seemed to choose the first drawing from each session. Looking with unusual eyes, Maurice could only agree that they were the ones with life. They rarely looked like Alex, often it was not certain from the slight distance at which he was sitting if it was a woman or even a human at all. Monsters indeed! André held out one that looked more like a tiger stalking through bushes. Maurice remembered the session, an early one when they stilled played together by the river, she crawling up the bank to frighten him.

The pile of drawings in front of André was several inches thick now. He was talking money, silly sounding sums to Maurice's fuddled brain. Alex was guiding him, arguing for him, bartering. Eventually it seemed a figure was agreed. Seven million francs. The cheque was written, Alex gave it to him, he pushed it back into her hand. André grasped his shoulders, planted a kiss on each cheek, leaving, saying he mustn't stand in the way of the future work.

"What have you done?" he asked the girl as she brought him fresh hot coffee, hot bread and jam. She laughed at him.

"He came while you were asleep. He said he'd heard of you, could he see your work. I remembered him from when we went to Aix last summer." Maurice remembered too, the man had his eyes all over her legs the whole time they were in the gallery.

"Maurice," she stood behind him cushioning his head against her breasts, her long red hair falling in his eyes, "the cheque is real. Don't you want the money?"

He did, of course.

He still had a bank account, in Aix. It was a long drive today, she at the wheel, he shaking again, unable to see clearly. She had helped him wash, found his best clothes, the pants without holes in the crotch, the silk cravat, his father's battered Panama. He was ushered into the manager's private office when the cashier saw the size of the cheque. After, they sat for a while in a shady pavement café, not speaking until he left her, briefly, to visit an old, perhaps his only, friend.

"You're an old fool, Maurice," he said "mais c'est entendu, I understand."

The forms had been signed and witnessed. He returned to the bank, took out the little available cash he had, and found her again at the café. She was sitting watching the old folk chatting on a nearby bench, still alone,. He ordered lemon tea, they would eat later, and drink, when it was cool in the evening.

Driving home she took the long way round, driving to the very top of the mountain. The old 2CV was high enough and tough enough, old enough too to know it's own way. They climbed the last bit on foot. The moon flooded the surrounding country in silver light.

He took her waist in his arm, waltzing her slowly round until they fell to the ground laughing, a tangle of limbs and falling off clothes, kissing deeply. He took charge. For the first time between them he led her, eyes wide, lips parted into a passion he hadn't known existed. They both cried out, sinking down again into the scrubby grass. The moon had left them when he roused enough to lift himself off her soft body. She was still asleep, a little smile curling her mouth. He rolled off gently, not wishing to wake her.

The ground fell away beneath him. He grabbed half-heartedly at a tussock then decided to go down silently. She mustn't wake, not yet. Before he hit the ground below he was glad he had left her this afternoon. The visit to the notary to change his will was just in time. She would cry, perhaps, but she was young. And seven million francs was a good incentive, he thought, for her to keep on living.

Black Jack Davey

The ale was warm as new piss. Jack spat the last mouthful away into the gutter which ran beside his stool. He preferred his own company to that of the other varlets in the tavern. They all were sparring amongst themselves over who had the best pickings from their meagre hauls. Penny pinchers, the lot o' them, Jack thought to himself, minds unable to think further than their bellies. Except perhaps once a week, he corrected himself. After sufficient ale and prompting from their fellow thieves, they would try for a lay amongst the town whores. Sitting out here in the moonlight, under the scraggy old hop vine beside the tavern's only sewer, his mind was full of another prize.

Why had he never seen her before? He'd been turning over the gentry in this neighbourhood for a goodish while now, albeit in a less violent fashion than the compatriots he'd left tossing dice at the bar. The pickings for a gypsy whittler were none too good but he made do by adding knife sharpening and horse gentling to fill out the gaps when no-one wanted to buy his carvings. Today was the second time she'd been down to the far end, the cheap-jack end, of the market, where he sat whittling fairies and jabberwocks and the cow jumping over the moon. She'd like that one. Asked him to do a larger version for her little son.

He hadn't smelled her at all the first time she'd come by him. Easy enough, one would think, to spot the difference between garlic and sour meat and the fresh meadow-sweet scent of a real woman, but it had taken Jack a couple of minutes to notice. After she'd gone he realised that his nose was still bunged up with the wax he used so he could sit between the pig pen and the old whore who sold posies of wild garlic to keep off the fleas. It was the only place the local men would grant to a travelling gypsy from the south.

The scent of summer meadow-sweet had crept up on him slowly, so engrossed was he in the carving. Eventually his eyes had noticed the fine red boots of Spanish leather, followed the call upwards over the heavy riding trousers, ochre coloured like rich earth, past the yellow silk of her shirt and the red lips, to stop at the eyes. Black they were like midnight, like his own.

"What is it you be makin'?" Her voice had the soft burr of southern women, an uncommon boon for his ears now, so far north. She seemed to be alone.

Jack leaned himself back a little against the crumbling wood of the pig pen, allowing his mouth to fall gently into a smile. She was a rare treat this one.

"'tis a mythical beast milady" he'd drawled back, allowing her to hear the southerner in him. "They call it jabberwock and they do say ... " he stopped, looked up and down the street before leaning closer to her, looking up into her face. "They do say there have been sightings of some such thing hereabouts, up on the moor and in the forest under the mountain."

He leaned back again against the pig pen, stroking the silky white holly wood, looking up from under his lashes to see how she took this, a smile half hidden in his beard.

Hands on hips, she tossed her head back, setting the red curls afire in the lowering sun.

"Be ye trying to affright me master whittler?" she laughed back to him. "'twill take more'n that to make me blench, an' I come up out the flowering dessert to live in this wastrel land."

He'd been right then, she was a southerner. But what was she doing here, richly dressed and in full command of herself? The women in the north were poor drab things, fettered as they were to their men. First father, then brother and lastly (if they were lucky) a husband who would outlive them by many years after scoring a brat a year upon their sagging bellies. The only older women were the witches and the whores, and sometimes a grand-dame who had somehow managed to kill off all her men-folk ere they got to her. Lived on and on they did, the grand-dames, gumming curses where there'd once been teeth and harrying the young wives worse than all the men-folk.

A tall shape came between Jack and the sun, casting a dark shadow on the fair lady.

"Come woman!" The voice was guttural but yet had some sweetness left within it. "I'm done with all this bargain and palaver. I'll get no more sense from the inky fingered fool today. Up with you!" He reached down an arm to lift her to his pillion.

Her chin went up. "I've not yet finished my business here" she replied.

"What business can a woman have in a place like this? You have a trollop and a drudge to market for you. It's already taken me too long in looking for you. Get up with you and away home. This place stinks worse than a midden."

She stood back from the great horse, looking up imperiously at her husband. His head ducked a little, his shoulders shrugged and a smile began to crease across his chin.

"I return to squabble with the notary in three days. An' you've a commission for this varlet give it quickly. You can collect it when I come again."

She turned holding out her hand for the carving. Jack placed the half finished jabberwock in her palm.

"I'll be back for this, master whittler. And" she eyed the amulet of the cow jumping the moon "I want a larger one of these. My son is teething and holly wood is said to ease the pain."

Jack turned to his bag, delving for a moment to come up with a disk of black ebony. Holding it out to her he looked full in her eyes.

"This is better milady. Perhaps milady will recall her youth and how the milk mothers gave us the night tree to suck as the teeth broke through the gums?"

Her eyes caught his and held them. "Right it is you are" she said. "My lord returns me here in three days, have them ready. I will pay you well."

Turning to the horse, she snuffled it nostrils with her own and, catching her husband's belt, vaulted lightly into the pillion, ignoring his proffered arm. Milord's brows beetled over his nose and he jabbed his spurs into the velvet flesh of the great horse. Mud and shit spattered up into Jack's face as it leapt away from the abuse.

Three days later the great horse shadowed over him again. Squinting into the sunlit halo surrounding the black mass before him he could discern her shape. Lightly she slid down from the pillion.

"I suppose you must await me here. An' I trust you to go to the tavern you'll be dicing with the lads rather than sitting discreetly by the wall with your sisters."

"No sisters of mine!" she spat. "I have my own business to attend to. I will find you when I'm done. If it takes you three times a southern man in hours to do your business then I'll ride the horse on the moor and give him joy of his outing. He'll get none from you."

She turned her back on him and made great show of examining the carvings. He jerked the curb, bringing a red froth to the midnight stallion's mouth. The beast rolled the whites of his eyes, curvetting backwards, only to leap forward against the spur. In a rattle of mud and dust the lord departed his wife, his own lip caught and bleeding between his teeth.

"He cannot bring himself to blemish my face and curves so my poor horse is whipping boy for me." Her eyes showed misery and longing at last as she turned them on him. Jack sucked gently on his teeth, whistling the out breath.

"I have the carvings for you, mistress." Jack held out the silver white tracery of the jabberwock in flight. The holly wood was fine and light, new peeled and still smelling of the tree that gave it up to Jack for carving.

She turned the little beast in her hand, held it up to the sun, watched the huge shadows cast by the tiny wings freckling over Jack's face. He sat sullen, sensing her pain.

"Why don't you ask me, man of my country, what I do here in this land, baring childer to such a one as he." The bitterness in her voice scalded him like acid.

"Why, then I ask it if you will have it so." He turned his back to pick up the fairy beast he'd been carving. His knife slipped, he swore as it slid easily through the flesh of his forefinger. In the instant she was at his side, snatching his hand to her, sucking the finger with her tongue rolling surely round the wound.

"It's long since woman sucked the poison from my blood" he said.

She did not answer, being busy at her task. His hand found its own way to stroke the red curls as she knelt beside him. She ducked her head towards his hand, dragging his finger along with her inside her mouth. Suddenly her eyes smiled.

"Come with me" he said, his heart leaping ahead of his head as usual. How else would he, a southern gypsy man, have found himself in this uncouth northish land?

"Tomorrow" she answered him, the words fumbling their way around his finger.

At last she removed it gently from her mouth and looked at the red slit where the knife had gone. Already the edges were closing and there was none of the puffiness he'd had last time he cut himself. She examined his hands carefully finding the scars of recent clumsiness, ragged white streaks ridged across his long brown fingers. Then there'd been no woman to suck the cut dry of the evil within, and she knew it.

"Are you still entire, man?" she asked him.

"Whole as new born" he replied, smiling now.

"Are you willing to take a woman who has born a bairn to a northish man?"

"An you'll have me take you out of here, into the sun of summer?"

She put up her face, drawing his head down to her and sucking now on his lips. The whore with the garlic posies, gobbled with her mouth and eyes to see such shamelessness. But thinking twice, as she rarely did, she saw her fortune in letting the lord know at some later date. But not right now, not now, let the pudding stew a little in its juice, it would then be riper for the lord to taste. The acid would bite his mouth and heart as he heard the words and maybe, maybe, he would need the consolamentum of a righteous whore, one who knew her place as his lady never would.

The lady sat a little while close beside Jack. Their heads were close together, the whore heard nothing more but she didn't need to hear. She knew with her heart when lovers tristed although she'd never seen it with her eyes. She watched the lady leave, the lighter by a well filled purse. But her hands were the heavier by two delicate carvings, a fairy beast and an amulet for her son. The cow's heels kicked up gaily as she did the impossible and jumped over the moon. Maybe he would remember and understand one day.

Arriving at the castle in the evening light milord found the courtyard very quiet. He left the black stallion from the dessert realms with the pinch-faced groom. The beasts sides were bloodied from the spurs and red froth caked the long curb bit, streaking up the tooled leather of the reins. She would berate him long and loud if she saw the beast before the groom had worked his magic. Despite the training his mother'd given him he couldn't raise the lash to her. Her horse would bear the brunt of his ill temper and frustration. How had she conceived a son of him? Whenever now he lay with her in the great carved bed something drew his manhood back up inside him. The hazy memories of their wedding bed in the hot southern night passed before his eyes like tantalising moths. Whenever he reached out to grasp them his hand showed only air, clear and transparent as her hatred of him. The red rose up before his eyes again. He could never make up his mind whether it was her hair in the sunlight or her blood. Slowly, he trod his way up the stone stairs towards the solar.

The fire burned sullenly in the great hearth, all the light in the round room came from there. There was wine on the table but no sign of her. He went across and out the door to the stairs of her private apartment. In the nursery the boy slept on, his tiny faced hectic and flushed but the miniature fingers were cold to his touch. Afraid now for his son might have the fever, he called out to her, to anyone, his voice echoing off the stone walls. His man came in furtively, shaking his head and twisting hands in apron at the fear of being in the mistress' rooms. No, he knew nothing of milady's whereabouts, he had not seen her since the morning.

The nurse followed hard on the man's heels. She tried a belligerent tone with milord at first. Taking lessons from her mistress was she, he thought to himself. Well he would teach her about that. Her hands left bloody trails against the stone where he flung her from him.

Finally the old one came hobbling in upon her stick, gnarled knuckles whitening on the black ebony handle. What was he screaming for she wanted to know. Somehow all the conversation was inside his head, he was no longer sure that any of these people existed outside his imagination. He went towards her, fists raised.

"Stand back!" she cried, raising the tip of her cane so he could see the discoloration on the point. "Too close and you will feel this in your veins and then there will be a new lord."

"Where is she? Tell me where she is gone!" he cried.

"None saw her leave" the dame, his mother, still held him off with her poisoned cane. "But I heard her singing as she went about the rooms early, just after you were gone into the town."

There was a knocking, his chamber groom came in.

"A woman, lord. A woman of the town." He stopped, hesitating in the company of the elder lady, and eyeing his way back to the door, fortuitously still open.

"What of it, churl?"

"She do say, milord, she says" he licked nervously at dry chapped lips.

"Get on man! What is this woman to me?"

"She tells, milord, how she saw the lady yester eve. In the town, milord, in the cheap-jack market with the peddling gypsy,."

"So? Milady bought toys for the boy" but his heart had stopped a beat, what was this?

"She says, milord. But 'tis true she's nought but a whore and who can tell the truth from lies with one o' they? Perhaps milord should merely beat her and send her away."

Milord roared, pushing through the door towards the courtyard. The chamber groom thought himself fortunate only to be slammed to the floor. He watched from there as milord took the stone stairs two at a time.

"She was kissing with him lord. Sucking fingers so they were. A pretty sight" she simpered into her jowls. "At least it would have been if they were true and wedded." She glanced up at him, peering through lashes caked with sleep and kohl.

After he had slapped her several times she got the whole story out to him. He left her.

She sat now gobbling in her throat beside the hearth, peering into the rushes and find the few teeth that had been left to her. Thinking to herself how it might be when he returned, for she was sure now that he would go, would hunt down his lady and kill her. The men were always fired for a lay after such a killing. Perhaps if she offered him the place between her legs he would also want her to anoint him and rub out all the sore pain in his muscles, from the riding and the killing. Then she would ask him, then while he was quiet and lulled with pleasure. Not many lords knew of the whores' gift from the witches, the gift of the consolamentum. It would feed the anger in her heart for the many lords who'd penetrated into her wise place and then forgot to pay her. This one had hit her. The lords believed all women were their right but now perhaps, for a little while only, when he came home again he would be hers.

Her heart had torn at itself watching the red haired lady, with her freedom and the man who offered to take her away. How many times had she offered Jack a posy in just such hopes for herself. Or at least of a little gentleness in the laying. And he had pushed them back into her hands, saying no. to burn out the pain that would be gnawing at milord's entrails, ah yes, that would bring the comfort of vengeance to her poor torn heart. She waited squatting in the rushes by the dying embers of the fire.

In the stables milord flung the saddle onto the midnight stallion, puled the girths and bridle straps tight, not waiting for the pinch-faced groom. The horse thundered out the gate.

All that night he rode. He rode up hills and he rode down dales, and across the wide, white mountain. And all of those who heard him pass whispered into their pillows "Black Jack Davey, that's who he's a hunting."

Dawn glimmered on the snow peaks of the mountain when he found them, curled together in a nest of new cut heather. Standing over them, his knife to Jack's neck, he hissed to her until she woke. The black eyes shone out like crystal through the red hair. She sat up laughing.

"Why d'you leave your castle and your lands? Why d'you leave your baby?" he cried to her, his hand shaking so he nicked the brown skin on Jack's neck. The gypsy, too, lay easy and smiling. Milord looked down watching her hands begin to weave the air in front of him.

"Why d'you leave your new wedded lord to go with Black Jack Davey?" He was pleading with her now. All the fire of anger was draining out of him and only fear and pain were left. She would leave. She would leave and somehow he would never recover. He shook his head at the crazy thoughts. Women, he told himself, were two a penny.

"What need have I of your silken sheet, the boots of Spanish leather?" She was sitting close before him now, her hands weaving light. "I have gifted you a child and paid my father's promise. Now I will go. I will return to my own lands, the Summer Country."

His hands fell to his sides, the knife to the grass.

He watched her rise and the gypsy with her. She went to the midnight stallion, touching his heaving sides, stroking his matted silken mane. As her fingers touched the ripped flesh where his spurs had dug and dug again he watched the skin fold back, the angry red disappearing, the flesh becoming whole and the black hair covering all. She went to his mouth and kissed the torn lips and cheeks. He watched her tongue licking gently into the bloody mess. He saw the meat and tissue to which his sawing at the bit had reduced the horse's mouth healing over. The sweaty sides now looked better groomed than he had ever seen them. The horse pranced a little, butting against her chest. She snuffled into his nostrils.

Jack, meanwhile, had collected their few belongings together. She mounted the horse and reached down a hand to help him up behind her.

"You are not fit" she said "to have the friendship of a beast. I claim him back from you. You shall walk on your own bare feet from henceforth." And he watched the leather of his boots peel away, leaving his feet white and naked, prickled by the sharp heather stalks.

He watched the horse and his burden dwindle to a dark speck on the far horizon. The sun was high overhead. Milord's head was spinning and his throat parched when finally he found he could move again. Somehow he found his way back to the castle in the evening light of the following day., his feet bloody through the shredded skin.

The nurse was there, holding up his little son. The child cried out at first and struck his tiny fists into his father's neck. Finally, however, he cried himself to sleep sucking on the leather collar of milord's jerkin. The whore found them there curled in the rushes before the great fire in the solar. She called the nurse to take the little one to his crib. Then she bent before milord and opened her skirts. Just as she had thought, he took her, and the blood began to run again within his veins.

After he had laid her, he stretched himself out on the rushes in the warm glow of the fire. One woman was much like another and this one moved and squealed in time with his thrusting. It was enough. Now she was here again, he could smell some scented oil close by. Rosemary was it, and rue? He moved enough to allow her to take the shirt from his back and pull his breeks down over his feet. She was whispering in his ear. What did she want? Why couldn't she just get on? Surely she looked old enough to know her business.

She was whispering again. Irritably he shook his head, knocking against her face. "What is it bawd? Can you not do your job without jawing?"

59

He could hardly make out the words, mumbled as they were between toothless swollen gums. It seemed she wanted his permission, why he could not tell. Perhaps she recalled him slapping her, wanted to be sure she was allowed to rub him down now.

"Yes! Yes!" He turned angrily onto his face. Perhaps she would get on now with less fuss.

Slowly, there in the light of the flames. She got the oil and prepared him for the consolamentum. She had had to ask him, he had to consent in the final act. She'd repeated the question three times as ritual demanded. His final rough "Yes" was signal enough that he had heard, that he had consented to the rite. She was well aware that he had not understood her question. That didn't matter, the witches had told her it was the asking that counted.

She began to stroke down his back, anointing shoulders, waist, hips and buttocks. He was groaning now in pleasure, at least she hoped it was pleasure but one could never be sure with men and he had walked a terrible long way home. The consolamentum would take everything away.

She turned away from him now, reached for the knife,, taking it from where she had placed it in the flames.

Sea Cave

The car twisted its way down the steep toll road almost by itself. She could not drive, some part of her knew to turn the wheel, change gear, brake, accelerate but that was not her. "Why did you abandon me?" the cry wailed through her head again.

She found herself in the car park, stopped, shut the car door quietly and stood fussing in her purse for the seventy pence parking fee.

"Who's there?" A light went on above and a head peered at her from the casement.

"It's Mrs Ash from Kitnor.

"Ah. I thought I recognised 'y. There's no charge for locals an' anyroad you live there now." The face was smiling at her now "You'm up bright and early. In a hurry to get there?" She still couldn't work out if the voice was male or female and the face gave no clues. "Be'y goin' to walk all the way?"

"The furniture's coming later. It seemed good to get here early and I wanted to see the dawn" she confessed. "It's the first day of autumn."

"So 'tis, so 'tis. I think I'll let 'y see it in alone though" the face was grinning now as if she was a small child. "Have to keep a look out we don't get no youngsters up to high tricks in the middle of the night but I can see y're one of us. I'm for me bed, good morning to 'y." The head disappeared.

Closing the gate quietly behind her, Gillian slipped into the dank stone tunnel at the beginning of the path nto the forest. It brought back memories of his face grey with pain matching the colour of the rock in which she found him. She emerged with relief into the light and climbed up to the valley in the sky.

Gillian stopped still for a moment before resuming her climb up through the dark trunks and the half-naked branches, feeling the forest surround her, enclosing, holding, almost stifling in its nearness. And then the forest accosted her, calling to her, sending the loneliness and recognition into her mind. The questions came again, beating on her mind.

"Where have you been? Why have you been away so long? Why did you abandon me?"

Shaking her head, Gillian realised she'd come further than she thought, nearly to the top. One more turn and she could see the tops of the chimneys climbing out of forest peering through leaves and the little spire of the church perched on its roof like a witches hat. She rounded the bend and ran down the hill to the track-way which led up to the cottage.

There was no-one here. For just this moment none but the forest knew she was here. Gillian savoured the time. Softly she made her way up to her own gate, passed through it and climbed the steps to her own front door. The key turned silently in the lock and she entered the dim quiet. It was truly quiet here but for the raging laughter of the fast running streams. Standing still, she held herself in her moment of possession and then walked slowly around the cottage in a dream, touching stone walls, stroking door frames, like an animal nuzzling against her master after years of lonely neglect.

A shadow appeared at her feet, "Agatha!" the cat purred in answer, twining her legs in long black fur.

"A proper witches cat, you are." she bent to stroke the soft damp head, the golden eyes looked into her own. The cat turned about and went back out the still open door, indicating Gillian should follow. Together they crossed the graveyard, climbed the crumbling stone wall to the path down to the sea.

"Be careful Gilly! The path's falling away down the cliff. There should be a sign!"

In her mind's eye she could still see Nick leaning over the churchyard gate to watch her progress. He had refused to go with her that spring day. Laughing she had clambered over the fallen boulders and brambles and gone anyway. Later, when she returned to him, they had making a pact to reclaim the land which was slowly slipping back into the sea.

"I don't want to lose you to a landslide" he had said, but it was she had lost him.

The white beards of fire weed and thistles now hung about the bank and clung to her shoulders as she passed. Ferns hid the edge of the stream but the narrow path was open as if someone walked this way now and then. It seemed it had been reclaimed, although she and Nick had done nothing to help. He had postponed their pact to the land until she had fulfilled the joys of following him on his travels.

The black cat stalked off ahead of her now, down the path to the sea. She followed, feeling as if she was in a timeless moment, simply putting one foot after the other without any need to think of past or future. The stream ran deep and quiet now in its bed of boulders, the steady drip from the trees was the only sound.

Coming to the sea cave she heard of the sea at last, so close, only half a mile from the cottage yet invisible and inaudible until now. The stream bellied out into a pool before scurrying down the gully of rock, full of autumn rain. Cat and woman skirted the pool headed into the tunnel which led into the sea cave. The way sloped down before them. Gillian could smell the salt.

Unlike the tunnels at the beginning of the path up to Kitnor this one was not man made. The stream had begun it, trickling through a fault in the rock until it reached the beach. Then the sea pressing from the other side, incessantly stroking the rock like a persistent lover until the weaker stone had given way, allowing a passage. Nick had begged her never to come here. The tide rose high, sweeping into the cave very fast before anyone would have the chance to get back through the low narrow tunnel.

She slid her way through the cleft in the rock along the narrow path, some three feet wide at best and barely five foot high and only inches wide at times, was always wet and slippery. The cat minced delicately before her.

The tunnel opened out in ghostly white and silver light from the crystal formations in the rock walls. Here was the tidal pool where the sweet water met the salt. The rock seat at the head of the pool was dry and clear. Gillian sat down.

"I'm afraid for you Gilly" he had said. "You can't swim well and anyway it's not a question of swimming, you'd be battered to death and drowned in that cleft."

"How can you know then?" she had asked. "If you've seen it can't be that bad."

"I've seen the sea come rushing up. It's so deceptive. For hours before, from the turn of the tide you can sit and watch it creep across the mud flats then suddenly it gets a boost and rushes the last few yards in minutes. Dad took me there when I was a boy, we waited at the entrance to the tunnel and then legged it as fast as we could but I was drenched and deafened with the noise of the sea."

She could see the sea from here, gentle waves lulling her with a soft hushing sound. The sun was sinking, barely visible through the low cloud wrack to her left. Was that the moon rising to her right? A silver disk hung above the horizon and she watched it climb the darkening sky.

Sitting watching moonrise had been all there was to do while he died. There was no-one to come, no-one to call, no-one to help. Alone in the mountains they had climbed too far.

"Lets do the peak before we go to bed, Gilly." He called back from up front as always. And, as always, she had followed him. The climb was easy enough, a goat path winding its way to the summit and there they had sat, bathed in the last of the sunlight, watching the shadows change on the mountains ahead of them, holding hands for hours.

"You're cold?" he asked as she shivered in his arms.

"Don't know. Just felt shivery. Hold me." And he did. They watched the red ball of the sun as it was swallowed up by the darkling clouds. Finally the light changed from red to blue and night took over.

"Come on. Let's get you into the warm." He pulled her to her feet and strode off down the mountain ahead of her.

There was nothing to herald it. He didn't even have time to cry out. She rounded the corner and there was the rock pile. She was completely non-plussed at first staring into the middle distance "Nicky?" she called "Nicky, don't tease me! Come back! Help me, I don't know which way to go."

"Gilly" the word was hardly audible but it made her look down. His head was at her feet, one hand was visible off to her left. Both head and hand were covered in grey dust, like a new carved statue. The lips moved again and she realised it was him.

They had brought no water, nothing except themselves. The nearest village was ten miles or so down the valley, walking the only way to get there. Their camp was just below but there was no help in it. He coughed up blood.

She sat in the rubble for over two hours helping him to die. She made herself leave him to get water from the camp. Tears had gummed his eyelids together with the dust from the rock fall, she spent some time trying to clean them without getting more dust into his eyes. He whimpered.

The moon rose above them, bathing them in silvery light. He waited and struggled with his life until eventually it gave in and let him go, just as the moon began to slip down the sky again.

A pair of yellow eyes watched Gillian from the other side of the pool. The moon was climbing here now. She got up and left the cave. The sea whispered along the shore, calling to her. She took off her shoes and danced in the cold wet sand.

Gradually the sea herded her back towards the cave. The shoreline diminished and Gillian found herself once again in the blue and silver vault of the sea cave. She'd left her shoes on the beach, not needing them any more. Now she walked barefoot through the pool and up to the stone seat. She was alone now.

The sound of the sea rose, a grumbling roar, the waters of the pool shivered in anticipation. Staring down into the pool Gillian could see the beloved face smiling up at her. She stretched out her own hand to take the one he offered.

"I told you not to come here" he said out of the pool. And the sea came rushing up.

Thomas the Rhymer

Rain smeared the green glass before his eyes. It'd been so all day. He'd come home from the fountain with the rain pouring off the eaves of his hat into the funnel of his coat collar. He was still wet behind the ears despite the dry blanket wrapped about him. Somehow he couldn't keep his eyes from the window.

But he had poured the water onto the green stone just as the old man had said he would. Now he waited.

The horse was weary now, the spring gone out of the delicate hooves. A day and a night in this lonely place took the heart out of him. The lady clucked half under her breath, chucking gently on the reins, allowing a little of the energy she stored to slide down the leather and the bit into his mouth. He tossed his head bravely, shaking raindrops over her face. The cold water refreshed her as the mortal miles clip-clopped gently on beneath her.

Tom turned away from the window to mend the fire. His clothes steamed from the line strung across the mantel. The logs coughed fitfully in the damp air, hissing now and then as water dripped from the sleeves of his shirt. Tom coughed too, a thin man with little fat on him to ward off the winter chill and it had been winter now for a very long time. Tom poked the logs into a spurt of life, flames scorched the hem of his trousers.

He hadn't been along that pathway since boyhood. But now the old man had died Tom's promise had been called up out of him again. Sitting now, watching the flames, he saw the green-wood path before his eyes again, felt the leather thongs bite into his shoulders as he had pulled the rowan sled along the frozen ground. Big though he'd been in life, in death the old one had been of little weight. Tom had pulled the sled easily. And when he had got there, what had he actually seen? The fountain still rose up out of the green pool, icicles fringed its edges like a silver shawl and the battered metal cup still hung from its chain. Nothing it seemed had changed.

He hadn't wanted to do it really, so he sat for a long while beside the green pool while his backside slowly froze into the mud, his mind leagues and years away. Then he felt the presence again, then the eyes, like stars, had shone out at him through the leafless branches. Stuck fast in the frozen mud, Tom couldn't move so he waited, turning his head this way and that as they drew nearer and nearer.

The fur was warm when finally it touched him and the wolf's breath was sweet as apples. Noses snuffled around his haunches, freeing him from the ice. Very, very slowly he stood upright. Bright dark eyes regarded him, grey paws circled round him, white steamy breath spun upwards and the yellow teeth shone out from the red jaws. Tom stood transfixed.

The old one lay lightly atop the rowan sled. Three of the largest grey ones took hold the leather thongs in their mouths and began to pull the sled deeper into the forest. The others stood about him but Tom had no intention of moving. When the last sound of the rustling snow faded from his ears the oldest grey one stood, putting his paws on Tom's shoulders. The warm tongue rasped against his cheeks, the tip stroked his eyelids. From somewhere a voice came into his mind, silvery like and singing.

"Wait yourself, mortal man, through a year and a day. Wait yourself and come not here again. Wait yourself until the birds call you. Then come and wash the stone for us. Wash the stone in the water of the fountain.

Tom found himself alone again, blinking into the last shreds of sunlight as they filtered through the branches. He shivered himself awake, rubbing his hands together and blowing on his fingers. Then he looked for the sled. Gone, it was. When he looked down he saw the snow all tracked about with prints, wolf spore. Beside his hand a few strands of silver fur had caught on the last bramble thorns. A voice seemed to whisper out of the tree branches,

"Don't 'y forget now Tom. A year and a day 'twill be an' you be here again. Don't 'y forget now Tom."

He stood awhile until the shadows darkened the path, then he walked slowly home.

Nearer now, she thought to herself, clucking to the horse. It took all the energy she could store to make her way across this land but the horse would do it. He knew the way, had made the journey many times before. Softly he whickered to her as she stroked the wet silk of his mane.

Tom's clothes steamed merrily and the fire sputtered its protest. It felt as if the mists of the forest were rising up in his small cottage. He pushed his trousers to one side and pulled the kettle on its chain over to the hottest part of the fire, he needed something to warm him from the inside. Then he turned back to the window while he waited for it to boil.

Something white glimmered through the streams of rain pouring down his window pane. He wiped at the inside of the steamy glass. Yes, there was something there, flickering in and out between the stems of the trees. It looked like a horse. With his nose pressed against the glass he watched it come on, closer and closer. There was no mistaking it, a white horse came out of the edge of the forest. There was a woman on his back, tall and straight, the rain seeming to slide off her silver cloak and her golden hair. Tom forgot to breathe.

Clippety-cloppety she came, across the clearing. Despite the darkness of the night, a light seemed to shine out of her and the rain burned with a silver light. Bright she came, riding up to the door of his cottage. Tom backed away from the window.

Knock, knock, knock. Three times it sounded on the oak that bounded him within the cottage walls. And again, knock, knock, knock. And three times more. The door creaked a little and swung open of its own accord, unable to resist. Tom shivered where he stood.

The lady stood in the doorway, rain streaming down her, the horses muzzle on her shoulder. Tom reached into his brown curls but found no hat to doff. He pulled the blanket closer round him and bowed down on one knee. She was the most beautiful thing he had ever seen.

"Come in!" he whispered, "come in out o' the rain."

And he made to rise, stumbling forward tripping on the blanket, dropping it. coming to stand before her as naked as a new born babe.

The horse followed her over the threshold and not a drop of moisture came in with them. Both horse and lady were dry and fresh as a summer meadow. The kettle began to whistle, Tom to blush and the lady to laugh gently as she touched his arm.

"'tis goodly to see a man again" she said.

Her dark eyes ran up and down the length of him. It felt like butterfly wings touching his flesh. She drew him to his own hearthside and sat watching while he brewed the tisane. He sat at her feet the night long as they sipped the warm honey water.

Drip, drip, drip. He could hear it now, there were spaces between the dripping of the water. Sunlight glowed wetly through the glass. The embers were hidden in the soft grey ash, soft and grey as wolf's fur. Sitting straighter he turned to face her. Her dark eyes shone down on him.

"Come and go," she whispered softly. "Come along with me Thomas." And her breath was sweet as she licked the night-sleep from out his eyes.

Tom struggled into his dry clothes. They were stiff now, dried hard in the heat of the fire, the trousers scraped his legs as he pulled them on. Boots, hat and cloak, he followed her out the door of the cottage. His hands nearly met as he slipped them round her waist to lift her onto the horse's back. She reached down a hand to help him mount behind her, then turned the milk white steed to face into the forest again. Tom never did look back.

They rode on and on through the darkling trees, the wet dripping never touching them, the red mud never spattering the white hide. The sun set and rose and set again around them before they cleared the forest.

In the last light of day they came out from the canopy of branches into a land Tom could never have imagined. Brown and hard it seemed in the last of the light, like rock that had been pulverised in a mill stone. Nothing grew here. As the light leached away he could no longer tell where earth met sky. Only the crunching sound of the hooves assured him there was any land left at all. He could feel the lady pressed against his body but nothing could he see.

They rode and rode and rode. Tom had no way of knowing time, his mouth burned and his heart ached. The horse's breath rasped in time with the rustle of sand about his feet. Sometime he could feel a tingling current flow into his veins as the lady touched his hand. Sometimes he could feel it flowing through the body of the horse between his legs. And still they rode, neither moon nor sun in the sky to light their way.

Gradually, another sound came into Tom's ears. It seemed a heavy rhythmic roaring sound, like some great animal sleeping. Louder it came, as they rode on into the darkness. Soon Tom couldn't hear the sound of the horse at all.

Then the darkness began to change, there seemed to be a silvering of the air about him and Tom could see the horse's ears as darker shadows against the pewter sky. There was a line again where the earth and the sky met. But there was something else too. Some part of the land between him and the horizon seemed to move, flickering, shimmering. As the light grew Tom saw the skin of the world heave and ripple like the skin of some animal when a fly lights on its skin. Tom sucked in his breath. The roaring sound pulsed in time with the ripples.

"'tis the sea, Tom she said. "Water, salt, and it goes as far as eye can see."

"It goes on for ever" he breathed.

"Nay, Tom. But it goes a long, long way."

And, as she spoke, the moon rose out of the sea and shone its silvery pathway to their feet.

"Does't y' see yon bonny, bonny road?" and she was pointing down at the pathway of light flattening out the waves and leading from the shore at their feet to the horizon. "The road that lies across the burning brine."

Tom nodded his head.

"That is the road to fair Efland that you and I this night must go." And she clucked to the horse, shaking the reins gently. Tom watched, unbelieving, as the horse set one delicate hoof after the other on the shining path. The light held them. They did not sink into the foamy brine. The light flattened out into a path before them and they rode on, easier now than all the days or nights in the dessert waste.

Tom's body swung softly to the easy rhythm of the horse's steps. His mind dreamed, hanging there in the crystal light, walking on water in the brilliant shadows of the full moon. The journey seemed one long endless night. In his heart he knew where she was taking him, hadn't the old man told him often enough? Had he ever truly believed?

He conjured up the fire light, the flickering flames, the hissing apple-wood, the scent of mugwort and lavender thrown onto the glowing embers, a cup of hot honey water warming his fingers. And the old man's voice, clear and melodious, like a great bell brushed softly with a feather stick. The rhythm of the voice had swung him along like the step of the horse.

"After the rains come" he would say. "That's when it'll be. An' thou'll go out in the darkness before the first star. Walk the forest path until thee come to the fountain. Tha know'st the cup. Take un, Tom lad, take un an' pour the water on the stone. There'll be great adventures for 'ee." And he would chuckle as he fell asleep.

Tom had no memory of how he'd come to the cottage in the forest. The old one told the tale of how this sorrowing woman had come with the baby Thomas snug in her arms, and left him there on the step. He was happy in the cottage, the clearing, the forest. The animals knew him. The trees would move a branch for him as he passed and always willingly dropped firewood. Bees made honey in the hollow tree. Foxes would leave a rabbit on the doorstep now and then, and the herbs grew in profusion.

The old man had given him books and cooking, geometry and weaving. He had shown Tom how to let the garden grow itself. And he had told the stories, sitting there in the firelight on a winter's eve, or in the bat haunted warmth of summer under the trees. Tales of how the land lived, the fey-folk, the selkies of the sea, and the seelie court. Tom had loved those tales. Folk dressed in silken spider weavings riding milk white horses, with the dark light shining out behind their eyes.

"When I die" he'd said, "when I'm gone and there's nought but the husk o' me left, then the winter'll come. 'twill come an' all before that even as I sink, an' thee must bear it for me. Take me outside" he'd said. "Build a sled o' rowan-wood an' cross the staves with hazel twigs, an' bind the wolf skin on my bed across 'em all."

He'd been pottering about as he talked, putting up the honeycombs to drain into the earthenware bowls. Tom had felt a chill cross over his heart.

"You'll have to tie me on. But I won't be no weight for 'ee to pull and the snow'll be down to help 'ee slide the sled." He'd turned to look at Tom's diminutive frame. "Ah! But y'll do't?"

Tom had nodded his throat too full to answer. The old man had tapped him lightly on the shoulder. "Ah! I know y'll do it."

Sitting by the fire together, around the longest night of the year, he'd told of the wolves.

"'twon't be this year. No. But I'm a thinking it may be next. I can feel them calling to me now. Stronger it gets as the light shrinks. They call me in my bones lad. My time is nearly done an' soon it will be for you to carry on."

"An' don't 'ee be afraid o' them, lad" he'd said. "They won't harm 'ee. They do come for me an' ee' must let them take me. Y'll go back home then, keep my fire burning for a year, through the darkest winter."

Tom wondered about the winter. They had winter, every year. Snow bright with robins, icicles making music as they hung from tree branches, frost stars on the windows. He loved the winter. But how the old man spoke it sounded dark, the words themselves carried a cold that pierced his bones. This was a winter Tom had never known.

"An' then the birds 'll come. Just when y' think y' can bear it no more. The black birds 'll come a callin' and' a callin' to 'ee. Hearken good lad, for that'll be tha day."

And so it had been. They had sat together by the embers of the fire. The old one had sung at first, gentle, silvery words that Tom had never heard before. The seven sister stars had shone out in the black sky above the clearing. Gradually as the sisters turned and set, falling down behind the tree tops, so the old one's singing ceased. They sat together in silence, even the fire was quiet tonight. And as the false green light of the first dawn licked at the window panes Tom had seen that the old one was no longer breathing. His lips were set in the slight smile. His eyes saw things beyond the cottage walls and would never look on Tom's face again. Tears fell down Tom's cheeks.

And Tom had wept as he asked the rowan tree for long branches. His tears watered the hazel as he bent to take the twigs she'd left for him on the ground. It was long before he could take the wolf skin from the bed. He spent the time curled within it, sucking on a piece of the old leather like a child. After three days the strength came back to him and he tied the wolf skin onto the branches, tied the old man onto the pallet. He watched beside the bier all that last night. It was then he noticed how sweet the old man's husk still smelled, rosemary he thought, and thyme.

As the sun cleared the top of the trees they arrived by the fountain. All the long path there had been in half light, glimmerings and dapplings as the cold wind shook the last leaves off the trees. The snow had come, as the old one said it would, but the days had been grey and heavy, like a darkling blanket cast across the bowl of the sky. This was not the robin winter Tom had always known. This was some great dark beast, hungry and malevolent, no lover of the little lives of the forest. He feared it.

The warm wolf fur, when it finally touched him by the fountain seemed a last link with the web of life he'd always known. It felt as if the web was breaking up on the old one's death and the wolf's sweet breath was a last reminder of how life had been. Now, here, walking across the silver sea, he remembered the bright dark eyes smiling to him as the grey paws circled him round.

Coming out from his inner world he saw the light had changed in the sea and sky while he'd been off dreaming. The brightness almost stung his eyes as he brought them back to focus on the world around him. It seemed there was another shore ahead, the moon-path led them straight towards it.

The horse shook his head and whickered gently, Tom heard answering calls from up ahead.

As the horse's hooves touched the earth again the apple scent rose up around him. Now he could see the blossom blushing on the trees. And he could see the rosy cheeks of apples too, peeking out behind the green leaves. The trees carried all the seasons. Tom realised how cold and frozen his body had been during their long ride. The sun was low and the warm land smelled of spring as he took a breath. He wondered when he had breathed last. Flexing his muscles it seemed as if a film of ice cracked off and the sun warmth was able to reach him again.

A host of people was coming towards them. Tom was almost lifted down from the horse's back, many hands supporting him, his feet unsteady, not remembering what it was they had to do. He stumbled, pitching into the ground, coming up with a handful of earth. Laughing, they took his hands and rubbed them on his cheeks.

"Now you're blooded to our land!" they cried.

The lady kissed the horse's nose before he was led away. She turned to Tom taking his hand, leading him across the sward towards the cave mouth. Such a cave mouth! Tom saw it fully now she had hold of him again. The cottage and the clearing would be lost within, he thought, you could put a dozen cottages inside and still lose them. There were things like icicles standing up out of the ground and hanging down from the roof, coiled and curled into fantastical shapes. As they came closer he could see that some of the largest ones were carved as well. There were dragons and unicorns, griffins and cats and all manner of beasts and flying creatures he had no name for at all. Passing close, he reached a hand to touch one. Hard it was and perhaps slippery. He put his finger in his mouth, there was a taste there too. The lady was laughing.

"Does't like our home then, fair Thomas?"

"Pick me an apple, Thomas" she said, and he reached up to the nearest tree. The apple came easy to his hand. He would have passed her the fruit but she took his hand and pulled the apple to her mouth, biting deep. Then she pushed it back to him.

"Eat it, Thomas" she laughed. "Eat the fruit of my gardens. It gives the silver tongue and the golden heart."

Tom bit deep, the juice running back down his throat.

"The like o' this I never tasted afore!" he gasped and, even to his own ears his voice was changing.

He was taken to a room within. Again there was a luminescence flowing out of the walls, lighting the place from within. Peering through an arch in the rock he saw a great bathing pool steaming. Flowers were strewn in the water, fresh clothes were laid out for him. The fey-folk began stripping him of the weather beaten clothing he wore, helped him into the bath, rubbed out of him the cold and pain of the journey in the warm, scented water.

Later, at the feast, Tom remembered little of the dishes, only that his palate seemed to be sung to by a melody of flavours, his ears fed by tasteful music, his eyes feasting on a symphony of colour and light. The winds blew summer meadow fragrances through the wide halls, spiced with autumn leaves and the smell of earth after rain. The lady took every opportunity to fondle him.

Later, in bed, it was the same. The dawn seemed long in coming and yet it arrived too early for Tom. His heart and soul belonged to the lady. Days passed in pleasure. When he was not with her he spent his time with the elves learning songs and the making of instruments. Soon he was called upon to play in the great hall of an evening. His fame spread throughout the seelie courts into the whole of Efland.

One day she rose early and he did not see her all day. In the evening she looked away from him often but was always ready to catch his eye should he look to her. That night their love burned up brighter than the day star at midsummer. When he awoke she was gone.

Tom wandered through empty halls. All the doors and passages seemed to lead him outside and, from there, he found no way to return again within. He sat on a stone where the cave entrance had been watching the sun rise and fall over the sea. At evening the horse came to him.

A little Elven lad came soon after, carrying a small satchel. The horse was bridled for a journey, the Elven lad tightened the girths and handed the satchel to Tom.

"Thee must return to the land o' men now. Y've done y' work for us here. The lady is abed now wi' child."

Tom turned about. The bare cliff confronted him, no entry now into the seelie court. He stood, totally bereft.

"Come now Tom. The old one told y' what was needed. He told y' how 'ee were born. Did y' think 'twould be any different for 'ee now?"

"I never did think" Tom stumbled over the words. "I never did believe. In truth, I wanted to believe there is no pain, no loss."

"'tis so for her too, Tom. The lady grieves for 'ee too. An' think 'ee, tha's something to look forward to. For her 'tis something to lose again. She loses thee now, later on she loses the babe as well."

Tom stood aghast. He had forgotten. The promise was the same for him as it had been for the old one, nine nights of pleasure, nine months of waiting and three times nine years of companionship. But for her, was it only the nine nights and the nine months and then the babe would be gone from her forever?

He mounted up onto the horse's back. The milk white steed shook his silvery mane and set off for the shore. Tom never looked back.

He had counted the days and now, when the toll was done, he waited in the shadow of the porch. The moon was full again. He had not slept now for nigh on a week, waiting, watching.

Some trick of light caught his eye. He followed the owl's hunting path round the edge of the clearing. She flew long and slow, silent wings cupping the air, a fleeting white ghost of shadow.

"Gwenhwyfar he breathed the owl's name in the old tongue.

She called, a wild shrieking cry, like an infant who leaves the safety of his mother's arms for the loneliness of cold stone. Tom shook his head, the cry ringing in his ears and driving dreams away. Looking down he saw the white clad bundle by the door post.

Crying out, calling to her, he stumbled through the door. In the gloaming at the edge of the forest he thought he saw the flick of a silver tail, thought he heard the rhythm of the hoofs on the forest path. The low branch caught him round the waist bringing him down and, as he fell, his eye lighted on the delicate hoof print fading now out of the bright, springy turf.

Slowly he made his way back to the cottage, to the whimpering bundle laid on his stone step. He pick up the babe. The eyes opened seeming like dark forest pools and he lost himself in their depth. A miniature hand grasped his finger and pulled it into the tiny mouth, sucked hard. Smiling, Tom took the lad inside.

Over the following winter he made the first harp, small enough for the tiny fingers to begin their learning. Every night he sang the old songs of Elvenhome to the little one in the cradle.

And every morning he sang new songs of earth and sky, of beast and bird, of plant and rock

Downtown

The neon sign buzzed intermittently on and off. Sometimes it read "cock", sometimes "ails", the "t" never made it. She was warm, waiting in the soft polluted air, breathing shallow but unhurried, it was an effort even to breathe. Her feet hurt.

Her face was invisible to him. This was an area where streetlights lasted an hour at best before some public spirited soul smashed the bulb, restoring the friendly darkness. The neon sign was tolerated. The outline of her shape suggested youth, she wasn't a virgin, he knew her too well for that but it didn't matter. He could wait.

A shiny sports car pulled up, very smooth. The door opened, Italian crocodile shoes were followed by a Milan suit. His slit eyes widened a little as he watched the shoes go round to open the other door. Very long silk clad legs above very high heels emerged over the door sill. They wobbled for a moment on the uneven pavement before they found their balance and clattered off towards the bar. The crocs followed. Still he waited.

She turned now, watching Crocs argue with the man at the door. Slowly she made her way over to them.

"It's OK Mac." she said, her voice was throaty, deep. And the doorman let them all in.

He leaped up and followed them, padding soundlessly through the open door. Mac seemed not to notice.

Inside was dark, smoky, loud, the pulse from the juke box vibrated right through him setting every hair on edge. Silk-legs was sitting at a table towards the back, Crocs was at the bar beside the woman. He slid behind a curtain, came out the other side and went to the bar. He ordered champagne and took the bottle over to the table where Silk Legs sat and stood a moment looking down at her. The body and face, now that he could see it properly, matched up to the legs and she was very young. There was something about the sparsity of makeup, just a dusting of pink at the lips and the soft mascara which made him pause. Was she? He would know soon.

She accepted the champagne looking over his shoulder towards the bar. He sat opposite blocking her view. Now that she had to look at him the creases at the sides of the eyes showed rising fear.

"I think he'll be engaged for a little while" he murmered, stroking the black gloved hand resting on the table. She didn't resist.

Leaning against the bar she smiled up at him, her black hair swinging aside to reveal very white teeth and violet lips. Her skin looked young and the breasts pouted at him through the dark silk.

"I like whisky" she said.

"Me too" and he ordered for them both. She was very small he thought, thin, with delicate bones. She leaned against him and he lifted her onto the stool, allowing his hands to slide down her arms as he let her go. She didn't resist.

The juke box rumbled into a slow deep rhythm. Rising from the table he held out his hand to her,

"Shall we?" he said.

And she got up to dance with him.

She was tall standing in his arms, he pressed her close against his body touching almost from neck to knee, his legs guiding hers in the slow shuffle of the dance. They passed close to the bar, close to Crocs. He could tell she wanted to reach out to him, stop, speak. He took her hand tightly, pressed his mouth on hers and steered the turn sharply so that Crocs could see her parted lips, hear the hiss of breath, smell her perfume. And then they were gone, on the other side of the small dance floor.

"I don't know you at all" she said.

"Would you like to?"

She didn't answer at first, able now to look over his shoulder towards the bar where Crocs was rubbing himself against the other woman.

"Perhaps" she snuggled a little into his shoulder for the first time. He smiled over her head into the mirror on the opposite wall, smiling that only he could see their double reflection. But no, she was looking back at him from the bar while Crocs set up the drinks again. She caught his eye.

"Who are you smiling at?" Silk-legs turned her head towards the mirror, the transparent skin of her brow wrinkled in surprise "That's funny … " she began.

"This is a funny place" he replied turning her one last time as the music ended so she faced away from the mirror. They had arrived back at the table.

"I want you" he said, holding her eyes with his.

Strange eyes she thought, golden, like an owl, but there was something different about them. He was stroking her again now, talking in that soft, velvet voice, her body warmed under his hands losing the chill panic of being left alone in this place. After all she hardly knew the other man either so what was the difference? And he had left her. This one stayed, gave her champagne, danced, kissed her. And he had said he wanted her. She stopped looking at the bar and caught his eyes in return.

Crocs was getting drunk. She liked it that way, they were much less trouble then, never knew what had happened, keeping the warm pleasant glow and the tiredness. They would come back for more and she was not greedy, would only take as much as they could afford each time. She was not one to rub out her market.

"Shall we go upstairs?" He slid off the bar stool nearly to the floor. She was surprisingly strong he thought as she half led, half supported him into the bedroom. Black silk sheets, of course, what else? Lying on the bed she stroked his hair, opened his shirt, it was all slow and easy. He wondered if she would expect him to make a move. He fumbled at her dress but she pushed his hand away, her mouth smiling again.

"Lie easy" she said "this is your treat."

His mind wavered on the borders of oblivion, some little part retaining consciousness and a watching brief, but mostly he wanted to drift into the soft rhythmic purring at his neck. It pulsed in time with his blood.

She had given her attention to him for the past half hour now. Sometimes they danced, sometimes sat stroking each other gently, sipping the champagne. He didn't like them drunk, it changed the chemistry and he always ended up with a hangover. She was ready for it. Standing together he slipped an arm round her waist, guided her out of the door, up the steps into the graveyard. Under the yew tree he laid her out on the marble slab, his fingers caressing the translucent skin where the blue veins showed through.

She realised that her back was cold against the stone but her front was warm where it pressed up against him. She felt like two people, in two places, ice and fire. Her own passion rose wanting him and still only his fingers stroked her in long slow passes. She mewled like a kitten feeling him lick her neck.

Later he carried her back to the waiting car, lighter than ever, unconscious, smiling. He laid her in the passenger seat, felt her pulse. It was weak but there, slow and soft, it would get stronger again.

He jumped slightly as she tapped him on the shoulder, turning he bumped his head coming out of the car.

"Need some help?" he asked her.

She nodded, he followed her inside, upstairs. She had rearranged his clothes, done up the shirt collar but the tie was hanging out of the pocket. Easily he got the man in the crocodile shoes into a fireman's lift and down the stairs.

"Thanks Mac" she said as they left, Mac didn't notice him as usual. She held the car door open while he slid the man behind the wheel, reached in a hand to find the pulse at the throat.

"He'll do" she smiled, and closed the door softly.

Together they slid off into the night and up the steps into the graveyard.

"How was it for you?" she said.

"Birthday treat!" he replied. "Just one of those sets me up for a whole month."

"Lucky bastard" she purred, nuzzling his neck.

They felt the cold wet grass around their ankles as they walked. Eventually they reached the yew tree. Standing in its shadow she took off her dress, kicked her shoes onto the path leaned back against the corrugated bark feeling it press into her skin. She was white as marble where the moonlight caught her, he felt his blood rise. He stripped his own clothes and pressed himself against her, for a timeless instant they were one being. Then they were rolling in the grass, laughing, playing, chasing each other round the graveyard, leaping the stones and each other, then falling in a confused heap of limbs to lick each other again.

As the first harbingers of dawn showed through the pollution clouds two black cats slid down the steps and over the wall at the back of Mac's place. They squirmed under the gap in the cellar door. Down below they would lie up in the earth-lined box, purring each other into sleep until the sun had gone to bed again.